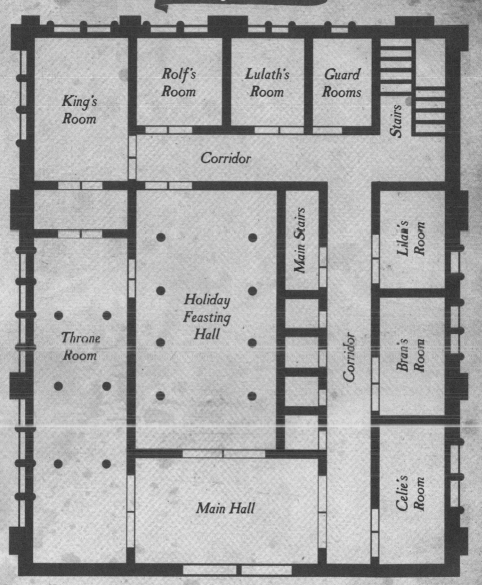

Thursdays
with the
Crown

Thursdays
with the
Crown

JESSICA DAY GEORGE

BLOOMSBURY
NEW YORK   LONDON   NEW DELHI   SYDNEY

First published in the United States of America in October 2014
by Bloomsbury Children's Books
www.bloomsbury.com

Bloomsbury is a registered trademark of Bloomsbury Publishing Plc

For information about permission to reproduce selections from this book, write to
Permissions, Bloomsbury Children's Books, 1385 Broadway, New York, New York 10018
Bloomsbury books may be purchased for business or promotional use. For information on
bulk purchases please contact Macmillan Corporate and Premium Sales Department at
specialmarkets@macmillan.com

The Library of Congress has cataloged the hardcover edition as follows:
George, Jessica Day.
Thursdays with the crown / by Jessica Day George.
pages   cm
Sequel to: Wednesdays in the tower.
Summary: Castle Glower's towers have transported Princess Celie, her siblings, and her pet
griffin, Rufus, to an unknown land. As they set out on a dangerous adventure to discover
their whereabouts, they find an entire lost people, divided by the wishes of two wizards in a
centuries-old quarrel over their beloved home—Castle Glower.
ISBN 978-1-61963-299-8 (hardcover) • ISBN 978-1-61963-300-1 (e-book)
[1. Fairy tales. 2. Castles—Fiction. 3. Princesses—Fiction. 4. Brothers and sisters—Fiction.]
I. Title.
PZ8.G3295Th 2014   [Fic]—dc23   2014005015

ISBN 978-1-61963-642-2 (exclusive edition)
ISBN 978-1-61963-742-9 (signed exclusive edition)

Book design by Donna Mark
Typeset by Westchester Book Composition
Printed and bound in the U.S.A. by Thomson-Shore Inc., Dexter, Michigan
2 4 6 8 10 9 7 5 3 1

Fondly dedicated to
Michelle Nagler and Caroline Abbey,
Expert Griffin Trainers

Thursdays
with the
Crown

Chapter

1

You are not leaving me behind," Celie repeated.

Rolf and Lilah exchanged looks, and Celie could see her brother and sister preparing to side against her. She braced herself.

"Someone needs to stay here with Pogue," Lilah said in a wheedling voice.

"But you could stay with Pogue," Celie retorted. "You don't want to get dirty hiking around the forest, do you?"

She knew that she had Lilah there. Lilah was already upset that they'd had to sleep on the hard stone floor of this run-down hatching tower last night. They didn't have any water for drinking, let alone washing, and Lilah was looking as mussed as anyone had ever seen her.

Lilah ran her fingers through her hair, caught them on a snarl, and straightened. "I . . . I . . . Listen to me, Celie," she said. "We don't know what's out there. We don't know if we're alone, or if there are people right outside this tower, and if those people are dangerous. We don't know what animals are out there."

"You think that I don't know that?" Celie looked at her sister in disbelief. Did Lilah think she was an infant? Not only that, this was the third time at least that they'd had this argument.

Here they were, in the Glorious Arkower, the land where her beloved Castle had been built, and they wanted her to sit. And wait. And listen to Pogue snore. Her feet positively itched with the need to get out of this cramped tower and explore—but no, it was not allowed!

Celie paced around the edges of the tower, which didn't take long, while Rolf and Lilah watched her. They were both working up more reasons for her to stay behind while they explored; she could see the wheels turning in both their brains.

It was true that someone needed to watch their friend Pogue. He had hit his head during the confusion that had brought them from Sleyne, which fortunately had been the only injury. They'd thought the Castle was trying to shake itself to pieces, or that there was a mighty storm caught in its walls, and then suddenly the tower that Celie, Pogue, Rolf, and her griffin Rufus were taking shelter in had been ripped free and brought here.

Celie and Rolf had looked out of the wide arched windows, across an expanse of trees, and seen another tower, with Lilah and Prince Lulath waving at them frantically from the windows. Celie had flown Rufus across to collect them, and they'd all spent a long, cold night on the floor, with an icy wind blowing through the open window arches, carrying strange noises and scents with it. In the morning, Rolf had announced that he and Lilah alone would explore the surrounding forest while Celie kept an eye on Pogue, and Lulath looked for water.

"Now Celie," Rolf began, "you are the youngest, so it makes more sense." He seemed pleased with this logic, but Celie was not.

Celie honestly couldn't believe that they were doing this to her. Celie was the one the Castle loved best. She was the one who had raised and trained a griffin. She was the one who had found the broken piece of the Eye and restored it to its rightful place in the Heart of the Castle, what her family had always called the holiday feasting hall. She'd hoped it would help the Castle, which had been acting strangely for months: adding new rooms, refusing to take away unused ones, even bringing a tower with a live griffin egg inside. But once the Eye was in place, the Castle had nearly flown to bits, and brought them to the Glorious Arkower, presumably to find the other piece of the Eye, which Celie had proposed the night before, and which they had all agreed was the right thing to do. And now she was the one being told to stay safe, sit quietly, and make sure that Pogue was still breathing.

He snored again.

He was breathing.

The truth was that Celie was terrified of the Glorious Arkower. She'd never even been outside of Sleyne . . . not to Grath or Vhervhine or any of their neighboring countries, and now here she was in a whole new world! A world where she and her siblings and their friends were strangers, with no clue how to find food or water . . . or a way home. A world where something, some threat, had made the Castle gather up every last room, corridor, and stable left in the Glorious Arkower, and plop them down in Sleyne.

What could threaten a castle? What could threaten *the* Castle?

But when Celie was frightened of something, she liked to face it head-on. She did not like to sit in a cold stone room and worry, but that is exactly what they wanted her to do. And to cap it all off, when Lulath had gone searching for water, Rufus had gone with him. Her own griffin had left her behind.

"I need to go with you," Celie said to Rolf, trying to sound capable, and not whiny. "We need to find the missing piece of the Eye so we can go home and heal the Castle."

"We can look for it," Lilah said immediately.

"What if Lulath and Rufus have gotten into trouble?" Celie countered. "A young griffin, wandering around with . . . Lulath?" She raised her eyebrows.

"There might be griffins everywhere here," Lilah said. "It could be that they've found a village and are getting help." Her face brightened as she hit on this idea. "Yes, that's undoubtedly what's happened."

"And if they were in trouble, I'm sure Rufus would be able to fly straight back here to you," Rolf said. "They're fine."

"Makes sense," Pogue suddenly called out, stopping mid-snore. Then he rolled over and went back to sleep.

Lilah and Celie exchanged worried looks over Pogue's head, but Rolf shrugged.

"Lulath said he'd do that," Rolf reminded them.

Lulath claimed that Pogue suffered from a cracked skull.

"He is needing the sleep, but not too much, and the quiet, of that a lot," Lulath had told them with his thick Grathian accent. "We must be waking him at that quarter of each hour, and watching to see that the breathing is clear. But of a certainty the swaying when standing and the sick of the stomach and hurting of head will soon be gone! And he is probably talking with strange words and perhaps sleeping while talking for a time, too."

That had been a great relief, as Lilah had been certain that Pogue was dying. Celie was relieved, too. She hadn't thought that Pogue was dying, not really, but she had thought that his injuries might be permanent.

Pogue let out another snore and Celie paced the tower again. It was a hatching tower, with just one circular room with a sloping floor and a trapdoor that led down a narrow staircase to a small door at the base of the tower. It had no furnishings and no coverings on the wide windows, but they were fortunate that, unlike the tower where Rufus had hatched, this one had a roof. The worst part about the tower was that it appeared to be dead: there was no friendly hum, no feeling of warmth coming from these stones, for all that this tower had been a part of the Castle in Sleyne barely a day before.

Celie stopped pacing and stared out again, looking for Lulath and Rufus, but all she saw were trees. Strange trees, with very straight, slim trunks, branches so evenly placed that they looked man-made, and dark-green needles instead of leaves. Away to the right there was something that might have been a lake or a plain, and beyond that, three sharply pointed mountains rose against a faintly purple sky. At the foot of the tower was a damaged expanse of stones that had probably been the rear courtyard of the Castle five hundred years ago, and there was a broken-down stable and the other hatching tower. It was all very horrible and bleak.

In the distance was a haze of smoke that looked as though it might be from a largish village or even a town, but Rolf had deemed it too far away to reach. They would have to hack their way through miles of forest to get there, so they had decided that the two of them were going to strike out toward the lake and hope that there was a farm or house hidden in the forest closer to the ruins.

And it seemed that by the two of them, Rolf meant himself and Lilah.

Rolf looked at Celie. His face was stern, and he looked as he had a year ago, when he'd briefly been the king in their father's place. Lilah folded her arms, looking very much like their mother.

Celie sighed and sagged against the window frame.

They both kissed her, then went down the trapdoor and out of the tower, leaving her alone with Pogue.

Celie had longed all her life for a truly grand adventure, but now that she was having one she found it quite lacking. Lacking in food. Lacking in blankets. Lacking in adventure, really.

After what she thought was about a quarter of an hour, but was probably much less, since time seemed to have slowed down, she woke Pogue. He sat up and talked to her for a while and she made him tell her his name and the names of all eight of his siblings, from his sister Jane Marie on down to baby Ava, to make sure his brain was working. Then she let him go back to sleep.

And she went back to waiting by the window.

She had almost dozed off herself, slumped on the broad windowsill, when she saw the other griffins.

Griffins.

Celie felt as though she'd been struck by lightning, and she could only gasp and stare as a griffin broke out of the trees away to the left, circled twice over the ruined courtyard, and then dived into the forest again. Celie screamed with excitement. She leaned out of the window, trying to catch sight of it again, when two smaller griffins burst out of the forest, chased by the first one she'd seen. The smaller griffins fled, screeching, while the larger one turned back and flew toward the ruins of the stable. It landed and went inside, and Celie nearly fell out of the window trying to see if there were more griffins waiting for it.

More griffins?

Her heart was racing. She gripped the stone windowsill until her joints ached, and she let out another scream. She had just seen three griffins! *Three!* She danced in place, stomping her feet on the stone floor. Pogue snored on while Celie jumped and clapped her hands.

The emblem of Castle Glower was a tall tower with three griffins flying over it, but until this last year she (and everyone else in Sleyne) had thought that griffins were merely legends. Then her stuffed toy lion, Rufus, had turned into one and eaten horrible Prince Khelsh of Vhervhine, after he had put the Castle to sleep and tried to kill her family. Rufus the Stuffed-Lion Griffin had disappeared, and she had found Rufus the Real-Life Griffin's egg some eight months later. Having seen two real griffins in her life, Celie considered herself to be fabulously lucky, particularly since both the griffins had, essentially, been for her.

And now she'd seen three more.

And one of the three was only a stone's throw away from her tower, in the half-caved-in stables. Did it live there? Celie wondered how many griffins were left in the Glorious Arkower.

Wizard Arkwright, who had come to the Castle to figure out why it was bringing the new rooms willy-nilly, had admitted that he was the one who had brought the Castle to Sleyne centuries before, because all the griffins and their riders were dying of a plague. Most of the riders who made it to Sleyne had died shortly after arriving, already sick themselves though they hadn't known it, and all their griffins had died.

But it appeared that Arkwright was wrong, or maybe he'd lied. The griffin in the stable was almost as large as a horse, and gleamed golden in the dim sunlight. The other two had been much smaller, and brown, but griffins all the same. Celie just had to get a closer look.

"Pogue!"

She jumped down from the window.

"Pogue, wake up!" Celie shook his shoulder. "Wake up a moment."

"Huh? All right?" Pogue blinked at her.

"I'm fine but I need to leave the tower," Celie said.

"No," Pogue said, more alert. "We're not leaving the tower."

He tried to sit up twice before finally succeeding, and Celie pushed him gently back down before he could stand. He wheezed and leaned his head back against the cold stone wall, his face gray.

"I have to . . ." Celie stopped herself before she said, "see the griffins." Instead she looked away in unfeigned embarrassment and said, "I have to, er, *you know*."

Pogue's pale cheeks flushed.

"All right, all right," he said. "But hurry and don't go far!" Then he blushed even more deeply. "I mean . . . be careful!"

"I will," she promised.

And she would. Just as soon as she had a look around that stable.

Chapter 2

Celie almost flew down the spiral stairs to the bottom of the tower. Outside she looked around for Lulath and Rufus, and was both relieved and disappointed when she didn't see them. She supposed it was better that Rufus not run into any hostile griffins, but she knew that Lulath would be up for the adventure of exploring the stable, and he *was* reassuringly tall and strong despite his fancy clothes.

She hurried over the uneven stones of the ruined courtyard, which she thought would probably go at the back of the Castle, near the other griffin stable, if the Castle were whole. It made her head feel funny to try to imagine the Castle all here, put together correctly. That thought raised another question: Did the rooms grow and stretch and disappear when the Castle was in the Glorious Arkower the way they did in Sleyne? She would have to ask Wizard

Arkwright, if they ever went home, and if he could be forced to tell the truth.

When. When they went home.

Celie stopped short of the stable, trying to peer inside without being seen. The sun was high overhead, but there was something smoky about the air here, although it didn't smell like smoke and nothing was on fire that she could see. The sun was dark orange, and the haze in the sky made it impossible to see anything inside the stable. Celie took another step forward.

A furious mass of golden feathers and fur exploded out of the dark doorway.

Celie screamed as she was thrown to the rough stones. The griffin stood over her, one talon piercing the shoulder of her gown, pinning her to the ground. Celie continued to scream and so did the griffin. It opened its beak wide and leaned toward her face. She threw up her free hand to protect her eyes, and felt the smooth beak smack into her palm.

But instead of biting off her hand—which it was large enough to do without blinking—the griffin sniffed her palm. Then it sniffed down her arm, tilting its head forward so that the round nostrils atop the beak could get closer to her skin. It sniffed her clothes, her hair, and her neck and face. It tickled but Celie was too terrified to laugh, so she just lay there and shook.

The griffin finally raised its head just enough to look at

her. Celie gazed back at the round golden eye, trying to appear friendly and not too terrified.

The griffin suddenly screeched, which made Celie shriek in reply, but she got herself under control again after a moment. There was a scraping of talons from the stable and then another griffin joined them. Celie turned her head slightly to look at it. It was smaller than the one holding her down, and moved in a more graceful and less aggressive way that Celie found reassuring. Another screech, neither as loud nor as menacing as the first, and the smaller griffin edged forward and also sniffed Celie from head to toe.

To Celie's shock, the smaller griffin began to coo, and rubbed its head against her cheek. The feathers tickled her nose and Celie sneezed, which startled them all, but the larger griffin didn't attack. Instead, it pulled its talon out of her gown and took a step back. It clacked its tongue at Celie, and when she didn't move it nudged her with a talon until she sat up. Trying not to make any sudden moves, Celie stood and the larger griffin started butting her with its head, guiding her toward the stable, which was dark inside and potentially held other, less friendly griffins. As much as she wanted to see how these griffins lived, she was beginning to regret not dragging Pogue along with her.

But the large griffin would not accept her muttered excuses and attempts to dodge away. It steered her through the doorway and into the stable. The light coming in through the holes in the roof showed Celie that it was identical to the griffin stable that had recently appeared in Sleyne, though in far worse repair. Also, this one was being lived in. The stall doors had been ripped away, and the stalls were filled with nests of bracken and grass. There was a neat pile of bones in one corner, and a pile of nutshells in another.

Celie looked around their stable and then nodded and smiled broadly. "It's very nice," she said in a bright voice, speaking slowly. "Very nice indeed!"

Did they understand Sleynth? Probably not, but hopefully they would interpret her expression and words as friendly.

The smaller griffin fussed around her, batting her softly with upraised wings that had a slight cream-colored pattern on them. Celie tripped over a stick on the floor and fell into the side of one of the stalls. She took a step back to brace herself, and something hard under her foot rolled away. She almost fell right on top of the smaller, gold-and-cream griffin.

"Oof! Sorry!" She caught hold of the side of the stall and pulled herself upright, then looked down to see what she had stepped on.

It wasn't a rock but an irregular chunk of crystal. It was probably clear, and had some green color to it, but it was so dirty that she couldn't really tell. There was a clump of mud and a dingy feather stuck to one side. Celie picked it up, intending to toss it out a window into the forest. Lying on a rock was probably uncomfortable for whatever griffin slept in that stall. It was so dirty that her palms began to itch, and she wondered if Lulath would find enough water for drinking and washing. She didn't want to think about what was coating that rock.

When the gold-and-cream griffin saw what Celie was holding, however, it hissed and raised its wings. Immediately the larger griffin came down the aisle. It had something in its beak and tossed it at Celie's feet before lunging at her, snatching the crystal out of her hands. It backed down the aisle, glaring, and hid the thing in another stall. Belatedly Celie remembered Rufus's fondness for squirreling away jewelry and other shiny objects. He'd made off with her gold circlet shortly before a state dinner just last week, and he'd shrieked at her when she'd retrieved it from under his bed.

She held up her hands, fingers splayed, to show that she didn't have any more of their treasures, then looked down to see what the large griffin had dropped at her feet. It looked like a dead rabbit, and she said a silent prayer that they wouldn't offer her some raw meat and become offended when she didn't eat it.

"Oh," she said, looking down at the thing. "Rufus."

Then her knees buckled and she sat down in the bracken of the nest.

It was her old stuffed toy lion. Here at her feet. In the Glorious Arkower. She picked him up with a tentative hand. *Rufus.* Dirty and a bit mashed, but familiar all the same.

Her eyes prickled with tears and she pressed Rufus against her face. Underneath the wild smell of griffin, she smelled home, and her throat closed on a small sob.

When she'd pulled herself together, Celie looked up at the large griffin, who had returned from hiding the crystal and was now giving her a decidedly pleased look. Her tears dried at once.

"Oh," Celie said again. "It was *you!*"

And it was. It was the griffin that had eaten Prince Khelsh! The Castle had traded it for her stuffed toy, or perhaps Rufus the lion had merely gotten caught up in the spell that had briefly brought this griffin to Sleyne and then sent it back to the Glorious Arkower. Celie held out her hand and when the griffin dipped its head, she stroked its smooth feathers.

"Thank you," she said sincerely.

The large griffin gave a pleased clack.

She held out Rufus the lion, but the griffin pushed it back at her with its head. She gave her toy a fond hug and thanked the big griffin again before stuffing Rufus down inside her bodice, where he had been when Khelsh had attacked her.

"I should probably get back to the tower," she said reluctantly. She pointed toward the door. "Pogue is probably worried sick . . . or maybe he's just asleep . . ."

She tried to sidle around the two creatures, worried that they would try to stop her, but they turned and flanked her, walking with her out of the stable and across the courtyard.

They were almost to the foot of the tower when she heard Lulath's exuberant shout from the trees.

"Our Celie! You are being the friend of more marvelous of the griffins!"

The griffins on either side of Celie stiffened. The larger one—Celie had realized that he was male, and the other female, probably his mate—half raised his wings in a defensive move. Celie had to duck to avoid getting a gold feather in the eye.

She raised her hands to try to make a shushing gesture at Lulath, so that he wouldn't further startle the griffins, and then Rufus came romping out of the trees. He took one look at Celie standing between the two full-grown griffins and screeched in pure rage. Celie took a step backward in shock: she had never heard her darling make such a sound before! Rufus raised his wings and charged at the male, never mind that Rufus was nearly half the other griffin's size.

The male griffin leaped forward with a cry of challenge, and Celie began to scream. She tried to grab hold of the big griffin, but he left her behind in two bounds, and the female promptly herded her away from the fight. Lulath dropped the bundle he was holding, spilling berries everywhere, and tried to wade into the fray. Even he, tall as he was, was quickly tossed out of the way by the male griffin.

Lulath ran to Celie instead of trying again. The female griffin hissed at him, but Celie reached out and grabbed his arm, which calmed the griffin down. She turned to watch the fight, and so did Celie and Lulath. Celie felt faint, as though all the blood had drained out of her body, watching her fierce little Rufus do battle with the enormous older male.

"Oh," Lulath said. And then, "Oh!" He grabbed Celie's hand on his arm, squeezing it tightly. "They are making the play fighting!"

"What?" Celie spared him only a glance, but when she did, she saw a smile spreading across the Grathian prince's face.

"Yes, yes! You are knowing that at times my girls, they having the fighting!" Lulath was the proud father of four tiny spoiled dogs. "They are biting and fighting and rolling and growling?"

Celie nodded, and then said yes, since Lulath didn't take his eyes off the griffins. The little dogs would suddenly erupt into action, leaping at each other's throats, snarling and nipping. The first time she'd seen it happen she'd been horrified and tried to pull them apart, earning a bite on the hand in the process, but Lulath had only laughed.

"Yes," he said, as he'd told her back then, "they are only deciding who will be queen for the day, and taking some of their energy and putting it to work." He nodded. "That is what these griffins are doing! This is not being a serious fight! The griffin that is so large, he is not hurting Rufus, but I am thinking that he could. I am guessing that this is being a test: Who are you, new small griffin, and what can you be doing?"

It was true. The fight was very loud, and the griffins

were flinging themselves about with abandon, but so far no blood had been drawn. Rufus's cries sounded very much like the cries he made during a rousing game of Kill the Leather Ball, and the larger griffin was almost chuckling. By now he easily could have pinned Rufus down, but instead he dodged back and forth and snapped at him without actually making contact. Celie felt some of the blood return to her face and hands. If this was merely some kind of griffin greeting, she could handle it. She still didn't like it, though.

At last, exhausted and panting, the griffins separated. Rufus drooped, and his fur and feathers were a mess, but when Celie ran toward him he straightened and clicked his beak. She threw her arms around his neck and told him he was good and brave and wonderful. The male griffin hovered nearby, watching them with one eye while he preened and fussed over the state of his own feathers. Lulath came over to join Celie, stroking Rufus and calling him "such the clever of griffins!"

This caught the male griffin's full attention, and he sniffed Lulath up and down. The prince held out his arms and let the griffin snort and bat at him with good grace. The female griffin joined them and sniffed Lulath briefly. Then she smelled Rufus, then Celie again. She carked a question to her mate, and he lifted his head and crowed in answer. The female froze, and Celie took a step closer to Rufus, suddenly frightened again. What were they going to do now?

The female griffin was buffeting Rufus with her wings, sniffing him and shoving Celie out of the way so that she could rub her head against Rufus. She was cooing, almost purring, really, and Rufus surprised Celie by making the sound in turn.

"What's happening, Lulath?" Celie whispered her question, not wanting to scare the griffins.

"Our Celie," Lulath said in a reverent hush, "it is my thinking that they are being the beautiful mother and the proud father of the beloved Rufus."

Chapter
3

The joyous reunion of Rufus and his parents was cut short when Lilah and Rolf emerged from the trees looking thoroughly filthy, scratched, and hungry. When they saw Celie and Lulath standing in the middle of a huddle of griffins, Lilah let out a scream that would have rivaled the most piercing griffin war cry.

Lilah ran at the griffins, her fists raised, which shocked Celie at first. Then Celie realized how this must look to her sister: she and Lulath were standing under the upraised wings of two large griffins, who were squawking and flashing their talons and opening and closing their beaks in excitement. They were butting heads with each other and with Celie and Lulath, which did hurt, but in an endearing way, like being hugged too tightly by a great-aunt.

"Lilah, it's all right," Celie shouted. Celie managed to slither out of the huddle of griffins and grab her sister's wrists before Lilah hit one of them. "We're fine! They're Rufus's parents!"

"They're what?"

Lilah drew back and stared, first at the griffins, then at Celie, then back again.

"His parents? That's amazing," Rolf said, running up. "Are you sure?"

"Only be looking at him, and looking at them," Lulath said. "Besides which, they are so very, with the excitement!"

"Oh, how wonderful," Lilah breathed. "Aren't they magnificent?"

They were. Celie felt her eyes prickle with tears again as she watched the two adult griffins cuddling Rufus.

Her family had always been very close. Her father, King Glower the Seventy-ninth, had never shied away from embracing his children no matter their ages or the formality of the occasion. Their mother was fond of grabbing them, even Bran, who was the Royal Wizard, and covering their cheeks with kisses. And since last year, when the king and queen and Bran had nearly died, they'd been even more affectionate.

When would Celie see them again? When was the next time she would be kissed by her mother, the way Rufus was being kissed by his?

The griffins edged closer to Lilah and Rolf.

"Now they will have the scenting of you," Lulath instructed Lilah and Rolf. "Do not be having fears."

But the griffins weren't sniffing them. All three were

standing in a line, staring into the forest where Lilah and Rolf had just emerged. Rolf looked back, nervous.

"Do they see something? I could have sworn we were being followed," he said. "Didn't I tell you, Lilah?"

"It's just because it's a strange place," Lilah began, shaking back her hair.

Before she could finish, Rufus's parents took off, leaping into the sky. They called back and Rufus answered. Then he cuddled close to Celie, who put her arm around him, glad that he still wanted her even though he'd found his family.

Rufus's parents landed again and were clearly calling for him to go with them. Torn, Rufus shrugged off Celie's arm and took a few steps toward his father. Celie tried not to be hurt by this.

"There's something wrong, Cel," Rolf said, putting a hand on her shoulder. "Let him go."

Celie nodded. She swallowed the lump in her throat and made a shooing gesture. "Go on, boy," she said gently. "Go ahead."

Rufus's parents flew off, and this time he went with them.

"He'll come back," Rolf said as Celie tried not to cry.

"Of course he will," said a voice behind them. "Griffins and their riders are bonded for life."

Celie whirled around and the others followed her. Rolf cursed and Lilah gasped, but Lulath said nothing at all, nor did Celie. She just felt the blood drain out of her face and hands again, and glancing up at Lulath, she saw that he also was pale. He very gently took her right hand in his left, then reached over and took Lilah's hand with his right.

Standing at the edge of the courtyard, in the shadow of the tall trees, was a man. A very old man. He had a great ruff of white hair like a lion's, and wore belted, dust-colored robes. He was tall with a high forehead and dark eyes that were very round, giving him a constant look of surprise. He looked familiar.

"Who are you?" Rolf demanded, throwing back his shoulders and doing his best to appear princely. He stepped in front of the others, which made Lilah hiss in irritation, but Celie was secretly glad.

"I no longer have a name," the old man said with gentle regret. "Long ago I was a wizard, but I have cast aside such things, that I may fade away with my land."

Celie felt one of her eyebrows rising, almost involuntarily, at this speech. Out of the corner of her eye she saw Lilah's mouth curl up in a faint smirk.

"I see," Rolf said, sounding just a touch nonplussed. "Then how shall we address you?"

"I may be called by the name of my country, though it, too, has passed beyond," the old man intoned.

At the words "passed beyond," Celie knew why he looked so familiar.

"You're Wizard Arkwright's uncle," she blurted out. "The Arkower!"

He looked surprised, and then pleased.

"Ah! You have heard of me?"

"We hoped that we would find you," Rolf said. "Your nephew, Wizard Arkwright . . . thought you might help us."

That was stretching the truth a little, Celie thought. Arkwright had had to be threatened and cajoled for everything he told them, and had said only that his uncle had the other piece of the Castle's Eye. They had no reason to think that he would help them, and it was only the greatest good luck that they'd even found him in this strange world.

"My nephew lives?" The Arkower's ancient face crinkled with pleasure.

They nodded.

The old man leaned forward. "And he has a griffin of his own now, of course?"

They all looked at one another, and Celie made a little encouraging motion at Rolf. As the Crown Prince, he really should speak for them, even though he was rolling his eyes at Lilah, who was older.

Finally Rolf straightened even more, brushing at his dirty tunic in a completely useless gesture. He looked like he'd been, well, fighting his way through a dense forest, and his clothes were clearly ruined.

"He does not," Rolf said finally.

"What? All that way and no griffin?" The Arkower clucked his tongue. "How unfortunate." He gave Rolf a searching look, then glanced up at the hazy sky. "And where is your griffin?"

Rolf shook his head slightly. "I don't have one. Only Celie does." He waved a hand at Celie. She took a small step forward, still clutching Lulath's hand.

"Only the Hathelocke girl?" The Arkower's eyebrows climbed ever higher. "Then you are not highly placed at court, for all your fine clothing?"

"I am the Crown Prince of Sleyne and heir to Castle Glower," Rolf announced, more than a little offended. "Princess Cecelia is my sister. She's not a Hathelocke, not really. She is of Sleyne," he finished rather lamely.

"Castle... Glower?" The Arkower rolled the words around his mouth. "Glower?"

"That's what the Castle is called, in Sleyne," Celie said helpfully. "I suppose it was called something different here in the Glorious Arkower."

"It was merely the Castle," the wizard told her. "The center of all." He was frowning, his eyebrows pulling down over his dark eyes. "But if you are the Crown Prince, why does your sister have the yellow hair of a Hathelocke? And why do you not have a griffin?" His mouth turned down and he squinted at Rolf. "Would none accept you?"

Celie let go of Lulath's hand so that she could reach forward and squeeze Rolf's. There was something about the way the old man said this that made her want Rolf to tread very carefully. Was he testing them? Judging them to see if they were worthy of the Castle? And what was he saying about Rolf? It sounded insulting.

Rolf squeezed her hand back but then let go of it.

25

"The only griffin in Sleyne is my sister's griffin," he said. "You helped to send the griffins and their riders to Sleyne, along with the Castle, but you did not go yourself. So I'm afraid that you do not know the grim news."

The Arkower cocked his head to one side in a motion that was strangely griffin-like. Yet there was something . . . awful . . . about him all the same, Celie thought.

"The grim news?" The Arkower sounded almost mocking.

"The griffins that you sent with the Castle all died," Rolf said bluntly, and Celie could tell that he was also put off by the Arkower's manner. "So did most of their riders. They carried the plague with them, and were gone within a few weeks. No one in Sleyne even suspected griffins were real until my sister hatched one this year. The Castle brought the egg from here for her."

"Where was my nephew, then?"

Rolf shrugged. "Elsewhere. He had decided it was better for all trace of the griffins to be erased. He removed any books or scrolls that talked of griffins and stayed far away from Sleyne."

The Arkower nodded. "I'm sure he did what was best," he said. He nodded again. "So, you are here to bring your griffin back where it belongs?" he asked Celie.

"No," Celie told him. "We're here by accident. The Castle has been . . . having difficulties, and we ended up here because we were trapped in one of the towers."

She didn't feel like saying that the Castle had steered

them to the towers, or that it was putting the piece of the Eye of the Castle back in its proper place that had done it. She didn't like this old wizard, and she wasn't going to tell him more than he needed to know. They'd talked about finding the Arkower, about returning triumphant with the other half of the Eye, but something told her this was not the time to ask the old wizard to help them with that.

"Having difficulties?" The Arkower sighed. "Of course it has! It's been under attack!"

"It has?" Celie and Rolf spoke at the same time.

"As has been the thinking," Lulath added.

"Why, yes," the Arkower said as though it were not a very serious issue. He seemed surprised by their reaction. "But it's not something that I care to speak about here. Why don't we retire to my home, so that you can eat and rest?"

Celie and her siblings communicated silently with looks and motions of their shoulders. Then Celie thought of Pogue, who probably had been sleeping all this time. Had it done him more harm than good? She'd been gone the better part of an hour now. Lilah kept rolling her eyes and making a crinkled face, which seemed to indicate that she didn't trust the old man, either. But they did need to get the Eye from him, as Rolf silently mouthed.

"I do not trust him," Lulath said in Grathian.

Celie was suddenly very thankful for their Grathian lessons, and hoped that the Arkower could not translate the words. How did he know Sleynth? Just another question, she thought, and sighed.

"Of course we don't trust him," Rolf said in Grathian, also catching on. "His nephew is a liar, and he's rather strange. But—"

"We need the other half of the Eye," Celie put in, taking a moment to be pleased at how good her accent was.

"But do we need to go with a crazy old man to get it?" Lilah demanded.

"He will have food," Lulath said. "I haven't found anything that we would dare to eat. I mean, I found some berries, but I have no idea if they're poisonous or not."

It always startled Celie to hear Lulath speak his native tongue. In his own language he was straightforward and well spoken. He never said things backward or left out important words, as he did in Sleynth. She wondered how they sounded to him, speaking Grathian.

"I don't like it," Lilah said. "I think we're better off on our own."

"I think that if we try to get away from this wizard, he will make things very bad for us," Lulath said. "Perhaps it would be better to go with him now, and pretend to trust him, and see what we can find out about the Eye."

"I don't like this," Lilah repeated. "Not at all."

"I don't think we have a choice," Rolf said. "Lulath is right: we need his help, even if we have to trick him to get it."

He nodded decisively and turned back to the Arkower. Celie wasn't half as convinced as Rolf and Lulath, but she had to keep telling herself that the Eye was more likely to be with the Arkower than in the ruins of the Castle. Besides, they didn't know how to get home, but the Arkower could surely send them. They would need to stay on his good side.

"We'll need to fetch our friend from the tower," Rolf told the wizard. "He's been injured and was resting."

"If you mean the pasty young man who is spying on us, he's just there," the Arkower said, pointing a gnarled finger.

They turned and looked, and Pogue came out of the shadows beside the tower. He looked sheepish in addition to still being very pale, though Celie did not think it was nice of the Arkower to point that out.

"I was coming to look for you," Pogue said to Celie when he had joined them. He had to lean forward with his hands on his knees and rest for a moment before continuing. "But there were griffins, and then the others came . . . I thought it might be wise to hang back." He grimaced and stretched his neck gingerly.

"Yes, yes," the Arkower said, beckoning to them with a curt gesture. "Now please follow me!" He turned and stalked into the forest.

With a few more uncertain glances at one another, they followed.

Chapter
4

Just inside the trees they found themselves on a trail. Lilah made a disgusted noise and pointedly shook her snagged and dusty skirts. Apparently she and Rolf had *not* found the trail.

"Isn't there . . . isn't there a town over there?" Lilah finally asked the Arkower, pointing to the west. They were heading north in an almost straight line from the tower where she and Lulath had arrived in the Glorious Arkower. "We could see the smoke and tried to find it."

"A town? It's little more than a village," the Arkower said with a snort. "And at this time of year there is hardly anyone living there but a few old people who refuse to move on."

"Move on?" Pogue asked, steadying himself for a moment on a tree trunk. "What do you mean?"

The Arkower paused before answering. He had made it

clear in the short time they'd been walking that he didn't like Pogue, or rather that Pogue was beneath his notice. He considered Pogue a servant and could not understand why they let him walk beside them instead of behind. Their protest that he was their friend, not a servant, was met with bafflement.

The Arkower finally answered, but he directed his words at Rolf. "Our people have gone to the West and built cities there, closer to the ocean. The griffins do not like the ocean, so we had never settled close to it before. This last village is mostly those too old to go any farther away, and those too pious to leave the Castle. Of course, during the holiday season, more come back for the tribute."

"The tribute?" Celie asked.

"To the Castle," the Arkower said. He gave her a narrow look. "I thought you said you all lived in the Castle?"

"Of course we do," Celie hastened to assure him.

"The annual tribute? The feasts and the decorations? They do not arrive in the Heart of the Castle?"

Celie stopped dead in the middle of the path. The others would have run into her, but they had stopped, too.

"The holiday feasts?" Celie's voice came out as a squeak.

"Yes, precisely." The Arkower continued to walk forward, and they had to scramble to follow. "Where did you think they came from? The Castle cannot make food out of thin air!" He laughed, a crackling sound that ended in a cough as though he were out of practice.

"We . . . we didn't know," Celie said.

When the holiday feasting hall—which normally appeared for only a week during the winter holidays—had appeared in the Castle that spring, it had been the sign to everyone that something was very wrong with the Castle. Moreover, Celie had been haunted by the sight of the decorations boxed up and stored neatly. Somehow she had always thought that yes, the Castle *did* make everything out of thin air, even though she and Lilah had had to live on leftover biscuits for a time when they'd been trapped in the Spyglass Tower. The question of who decorated the hall and prepared the feasts had plagued Celie since the Castle had begun acting strangely. Who were the people behind it all? Did they know about the Glowers? About Sleyne? And why were they doing this?

Now she had answers, of a sort.

"They pay tribute . . . to the Castle?" Rolf said. "Why?"

"The Castle was once all," the Arkower said, and his voice was almost savage. Celie drew back so that she was walking behind Lulath. "The center of our world. Then it was taken from us!"

"By the Hathelockes?" Pogue asked.

The Arkower paused again. "It was taken from us," he finally repeated.

They walked in silence for a while, and Celie tried to ignore the gnawing pain in her empty stomach. Lulath kept pointing out berries and nuts as they passed, but the Arkower would only glance at them and say no. He didn't clarify whether they were poisonous or merely tasted bad; he just said no and walked on. They continued to trudge after the Arkower, trying not to count the hours since they had last eaten.

Finally they left the forest and walked across a stretch of low, flat grass to a beautiful sandy shore. Ahead of them lay a lake, a flat circle of dark blue, nestled within a ring of white sand. The forest also stretched around the lake, but on the opposite side were three conical mountains that almost appeared to have been sculpted, not made by nature. There was a broad, flat boat pulled up on the shore in front of them.

"Well, at least we won't die of thirst," Lilah grumbled.

The Arkower whipped around. "Do not drink this water!" He pointed a long knobby finger at her face, making Lilah leap back with a frightened cry. "Do not even touch it!"

Celie rushed forward and took Lilah's arm, and her sister clung to her. Celie realized that she was shaking, her heart pounding. The Arkower's face . . . she wished she'd listened to Lilah and refused to follow the wizard into the forest.

"Why not?" Pogue asked. "Is it sacred?" He sounded just faintly mocking.

"Sacred?" The Arkower gave him an evil look. "Try *poisoned*, boy."

They all gaped, except for Lulath, who now turned facetious. Or so Celie thought. With his accent it was hard to tell, and he was so rarely rude that she had some doubts.

"There is being a way of having the poison to fill a very lake?" He shook his head. "What a wonder is this Glorious Arkower! I am so very! Never have I heard of such a thing as being a lake of poison entire!"

The look the Arkower had given Pogue was nothing compared to the scorching look he now gave Lulath. He, too, seemed to think that Lulath was making fun.

"It was poisoned by wizards," he snapped. "This is what caused the plague that killed most of my people and our griffins!"

Lulath drew back as if slapped. Lilah lifted her skirts a little and looked anxiously for puddles, and Celie scanned the skies. What if Rufus chose now to return to her? Did his family know about the lake? What if they followed her here and they all drank? She shuddered.

"Don't worry," the Arkower told her. "The native griffins know. They will keep your beast away from the lake."

Celie shuddered again, and added another question to the dozens turning over and over in her head already. How had the Arkower known what she was thinking? Could he read minds?

He went to the boat and began to move it down the shore, surprisingly spry for a man of his age. It dawned on Celie that he must be close to seven hundred years old, if what Arkwright had told them about his uncle was true.

"Come and help me," he called back to them. "We will take the boat along the shore to my home."

Rolf walked over to the boat but didn't stoop down to help the old man.

"Why?" Rolf asked.

"What?" The Arkower straightened, a look of astonishment on his face.

"Why are we going to your home, and away from the Castle ruins?" Rolf folded his arms. "I'm sorry, we were just so caught up in meeting you . . ." He stopped and cleared his throat. Celie gave him a little jab in the back to make him continue. "Can you get us back to Sleyne?"

"I *am* a wizard," the Arkower said. "But I will need things from my home, and you need food and better shelter than that old hatching tower can provide."

"Oh, yes, of course, thank you," Rolf said. He gave an apologetic smile to the old man, who didn't return it. Rolf stooped and helped launch the boat.

"Get in now," the Arkower instructed them. "Any farther and your feet will get wet, and you will sorely regret it."

They all climbed in, except for Rolf and Pogue, who insisted on shoving the boat out just a little farther. Right before the still water touched their boots they both leaped in. The Arkower passed around long oars, and they used them to push off from the shore entirely. Celie and Lilah sat in the middle, nervously watching to make sure the rowers didn't splash anyone with their oars. For a little while they used them as poles, pushing off the bottom of the lake and away from the shore. Then at the Arkower's instruction they began to row.

"How did you get here by yourself?" Rolf asked the Arkower with a grunt.

Pogue looked like he was about to fall over, and Lilah rose and took his oar. He tried to protest, but in the end he just nodded and slumped down by Celie. He still looked terrible, with a swollen lump on his temple and a grayish tinge to his skin. He gave Celie a weak smile and then rested his head on his knees.

"I was not alone," the Arkower said. "I have those who help me."

"Where are they being at this moment?" Lulath asked.

"They are fetching me some things," the Arkower said. "They can walk back."

Celie thought this was a bit rude, but she didn't say anything. It was cold out on the lake, and Pogue had fallen asleep again and was shivering. She got up and went to Lilah, who was the only one of them wearing anything approaching a cloak. Lilah's gown had a stiff little decorative cape pinned to the shoulders. It didn't look warm, but it was better than nothing.

After Celie pointed to Pogue, who was visibly shaking, Lilah didn't need to be told anything else. She handed her oar to Celie and unfastened the gold clasps at her shoulders. Handing over the cape, Lilah took back her oar, and Celie went to Pogue, smoothing the fabric over his broad shoulders as best she could.

It had a strange pattern on it: asymmetrical and embroidered, almost like one of the older tapestries. There was a violet-colored circle in the middle, a row of triangles across the top, dark lines down the sides, and two gray figures that looked like towers. It wasn't Lilah's usual mode of dress, but it—along with the blue velvet that made up Lilah's and Celie's gowns—had been found in a room full of fabric that the Castle had recently brought to Sleyne. Lilah had seen this type of cape in a book of patterns among the fabric, and though it was apparently a fashion from centuries ago in the Glorious Arkower, Lilah had decided that she liked it, and ordered it made from this oddly embroidered piece.

Spread flat across Pogue's back the pattern looked even more familiar. Celie studied it again. It looked like something . . . a map! She had seen a beautifully inlaid wood map in the new map room at the Castle a few days ago that looked just like this. How strange, Celie thought. Here was the same map again, only this time in fabric.

She felt eyes on her and looked up to find the Arkower watching her. Behind him the three mountains rose into the sky. She glanced again at the cape. Three mountains, above a circle—the lake! The Arkower was still looking at her, so she gave him an innocent look and turned away from the cape, gazing at the shore instead.

Once she had looked away from the cape and the wizard, she found the shore more than captured her attention. There were griffins diving in and out of the trees, and one walked to the edge of the water to stare at them as well.

"So many griffins," Celie said, startled. "I thought all the living ones were sent to Sleyne."

37

"Those are wild griffins," the Arkower said, dismissing them with a gesture. "They are too small for a grown man to ride and not smart enough to be trained, either. You can tell them even from this distance by their brown coloration."

"Oh," Celie said. The griffins that Rufus's father had chased away earlier that day had been brown. They must have been wild griffins encroaching on his territory. "But what about Rufus's parents? They're not wild . . . ?"

"Of course not. They're royal griffins," the Arkower said.

"Royal griffins?" Rolf asked before Celie could.

"The griffins bred and raised to carry riders," the Arkower told them. "The Builder's grandfather bred them from wild griffins, but by the time of my youth, they were as different as goats and sheep."

"The Builder?" Celie asked before Rolf did this time.

"Of the Castle," the Arkower said, looking appalled. "Did my nephew tell you nothing?"

"Nothing that we didn't wring out of him," Rolf said in a bitter voice.

"Well," the Arkower said after a momentary pause, "I am sure that he had his reasons."

"They weren't very good ones," Rolf muttered.

"We are almost there," the Arkower told them.

They had been hugging the shore, and they were almost to where the trees thinned out and the base of the first mountain rose up. The Arkower guided them farther

38

out into the lake so that they could cut straight to the base of the mountain.

Celie gently shook Pogue awake. He almost fell over, and was even more embarrassed when he discovered himself draped in Lilah's cape while she did the rowing for him. He seemed not to remember handing her his oar, which worried them all, but the sight of the mountain looming overhead pushed other thoughts aside.

"That is being a most very mountain of alarm," Lulath said, which was more or less what Celie had been thinking.

It was nearly black in color, and nothing grew on its sides. The side facing them still appeared to be too smooth to be natural—more so, now that it was seen up close. But any trepidation about journeying into the mountain was wiped from Celie's thoughts when a familiar figure swooped down and landed on the beach in front of them.

"Rufus!" Celie shouted with joy, which quickly turned to fright. "Don't touch the water!"

Chapter
5

Celie leaped out of the boat with Rolf and Lulath, holding her skirts high to avoid the water. She used Rufus's harness to lead him toward the mountain while her brother and their friend pulled the boat to shore. Rufus's parents landed beside them, clucking and snuffling at Celie, but as soon as the Arkower had tied the boat to a post they took off again. Celie and Lilah exchanged a look, and Rolf made a small noise in his throat.

There was something off about the Arkower, and they all felt it, even the griffins. But if he could get them back to Sleyne, Celie supposed they would just have to put up with him. If things went well it would only be another day at the most until they were home. Or so she hoped.

"Through here," the Arkower said, and led them to an archway set into the base of the mountain.

Celie had no desire to follow this strange wizard into a

cave, and she could tell that the others didn't, either. But again they looked at one another, and again they realized that they had no choice. Rolf and Lulath went first, with Lilah in the middle and Celie and Rufus walking with Pogue, ready at any moment to bolt.

But the inside of the mountain was nothing like Celie had expected.

It was like nothing she'd ever seen before. Turning in circles to look all around her, she could only gape, along with the others. The Arkower smiled indulgently at them, a ball of bright-blue light floating above one hand to guide them.

The mountain was hollow, or at least, it had been hollowed out. The rock had been carved into terraces and ramps that wound up as far as Celie could see in the Arkower's bluish wizard-light. Rufus cawed, and the sound echoed around them: the entire mountain was empty.

"Once, children, this housed five hundred griffins," the Arkower told them. "And their riders, the riders' families, their servants, and so on. Now only I reside within, I and a mere handful of attendants."

He sounded unutterably sad, and Celie felt sorry for him. She could see that her sister did, too. Lulath looked impressed, but also slightly suspicious.

"The solid stone that formed the inside of the mountain, the heartstone, was carved out by the Builder to craft the Castle," the Arkower explained. "And the outside of all three mountains was used to make the courtyard and outer

41

walls of the Castle. That is why the mountains are so uniform in shape now. These mountains are called the Griffin's Claws and are said to have magical properties."

"I'm guessing they do," Rolf said drily. "Considering that Castle Glower is what it is." But then he scuffed his foot along the stone and whistled.

Celie sucked in a breath. So this was where the stone of the Castle had come from. The blue wizard-light made it appear green, but looking carefully she could see that it was the pale gold color of the Castle. She reached out and touched one of the walls, and thought she felt, just faintly, a tiny hum.

"Castle Glower was really made out of these mountains?" Lilah asked in awe. Her head was tilted back, looking up at the carved interior.

"Indeed," the Arkower said.

Celie thought that he flinched a little at the name Glower, but she didn't have much time to decide. The Arkower led them to a ramp that spiraled upward, and they began to climb. Rufus's claws slipped on the worn stone, and Celie leaned on his back to give him some additional weight to help anchor him in place.

"I am sorry if your beast is struggling, Princess Cecelia," the Arkower called back as they plodded on. "Once, long ago, the ramps were packed with earth and planted with soft moss, which helped the animals to keep their footing, and was delightfully soft on human feet as well. But no more!"

"Why didn't you replant the moss?" Lilah asked, but the Arkower appeared not to have heard her.

Lilah raised one eyebrow, and Celie nodded. Here was yet another question that the Arkower hadn't answered. Nevertheless they continued to follow him. Celie held out a small hope that they would, eventually, get some answers. Besides, where else would they go?

"Do you feel anything?" Lilah whispered to Celie. "Anything like the Castle?"

"I think so," Celie whispered back.

The hum wasn't quite there, but she had a feeling like she was back in the Castle, if she didn't look around too carefully. She'd almost convinced herself that it was all in her imagination, though, until Lilah said something.

After climbing for what seemed like hours, they came to the top of the ramp. There they found themselves in a great, round room, the vaulted ceiling carved with images of griffins and riders, and a hole in the middle of the floor, surrounded by a carved railing, that allowed one to look down into the depths of the mountain. There was furniture scattered about: this was the Arkower's home.

"Please, be welcome, children!" The Arkower gestured for them to sit in some of the strangely shaped chairs. They were square, with low backs and legs shaped like Xs. Celie and the others looked around, then Rolf shrugged and flopped into a chair. Celie sank down into another, weak from not eating, and Rufus arranged himself at her feet.

The Arkower went to a large bronze bell that hung from

the ceiling and hit it with a mallet that dangled from a ribbon beside it. Rufus reared up at the sound, and Pogue gripped his head as though it were going to split in two as the sound reverberated throughout the mountain.

As soon as the sound died away, a young man no older than Rolf appeared from a curtained doorway. He was a little shorter than Rolf, but with dark hair and eyes not unlike those of Celie's brother. He froze, his mouth open to say something to the Arkower, when he saw them. His eyes went to Rufus and stayed there.

"Food, Darryn," the Arkower said without even looking at the boy.

"Who are they?" Darryn said. "Why do they . . . how did they get a griffin?"

"They've come a long way," the Arkower said. "And they need food. Bring it, and when there is time I will tell you where the griffin is from."

Darryn swallowed a retort and ducked back through the curtain while the Glower children and their friends exchanged uneasy glances. They had all taken seats, and Pogue looked done in by the long hike up the spiral ramp, but Rolf looked ready to flee at any moment, and Celie kept one hand on Rufus's harness.

A few minutes later Darryn reappeared and sullenly laid out a platter of bread and cheese, bowls of strange fruit, and a pitcher of fruit juice and cups. He hovered near the Arkower's chair, but the Arkower waved him out without saying anything. Glaring, the young man left.

"Please, eat," the Arkower said.

Celie knew that they should be polite and wait for their host, but the Arkower just sat there with his hands clasped, staring at a tapestry on the wall. She shrugged, and lunged for the bread at the same time as Rolf. They nearly knocked their heads together, and Lilah clucked her tongue, but it didn't stop her from hacking an enormous chunk off the cheese and shoving it into her mouth almost whole.

Pogue didn't seem all that hungry, but Lulath urged him to eat, and he took a slice of bread and some small, round green fruits.

"The brain is needing the food, friend Pogue," Lulath told him. "For the making of wellness once more."

"Is he badly injured?" the Arkower asked, without much interest.

"He is hitting this his head when the Castle is so suddenly bringing us to here," Lulath explained.

"I still don't understand why that happened," the Arkower said, giving Celie a narrow look. "Why you? Why now?"

Celie swallowed her mouthful of bread and cheese. "The Castle was in distress," she told him. "We should be asking you what happened! It started bringing in new rooms, rooms none of us had ever seen before, or rooms that weren't supposed to be there, like the holi—the Heart. Something must have happened here to make it do that."

"It brought us here because of you and your nephew," Rolf said, rather brusquely. "You and your nephew broke the

Eye of the Castle, and he hid it away. When we brought the piece back to the Heart it woke the Castle up. The Castle threw some sort of temper tantrum and sent us here. We don't know why."

The Arkower gazed at him in astonishment. "You think I am to blame for your predicament? It sounds as though you made a muddle of things just fine by yourselves." He held a hand up to forestall Rolf's retort. "But as for why the Castle appeared to be 'in distress,' as you put it . . ." He sighed heavily. "That I can tell you: the missing piece of the Eye was stolen."

Celie nearly bit her tongue at this news. She was eating more of the sweet green fruits and feeding bread to Rufus, and he almost bit her finger, too, she was so distracted.

"Someone stole the piece of the Eye?" she repeated.

Her heart sank. Now it would take them even longer to find the piece of the Eye—if they even could—and get home to Sleyne. She wanted so badly to make the Castle whole again! But if the rest of the Eye was stolen, and even the Arkower didn't know where it was . . . there was probably no point in Celie and her companions trying to find it.

"When we first sent the Castle to Sleyne someone took the remaining piece of the Eye away for safekeeping," the Arkower said. "One could almost call it stealing, except that at the time I thought guarding the piece seemed like a fine thing to keep this particular person out of the way. But he refused to tell me where it was hidden, and I only recently found it by accident. No sooner had I brought it here than it was stolen from me, so I guess the old fool was right—he was a better guardian than I." The Arkower almost seemed to be talking to himself.

"Do you know who stole it?" Lilah asked.

"No, but I know where it must be now," the Arkower told her.

"Where?" Celie leaned forward, dropping the rest of her fruit for Rufus to eat. "We'll help you get it back."

The Arkower shook his head at her. "Don't you see? It must be in Sleyne now. That's why the Castle is acting so strangely." He shrugged. "It must have been in one of the rooms the Castle hadn't sent to Sleyne before."

"We've explored those rooms from top to bottom," Pogue argued. "I've gone over every inch of them myself with the Royal Wizard. There's nothing that would be a broken piece of the Eye."

"Clearly you didn't look hard enough," the Arkower said, and returned to contemplating the tapestry.

Celie and the others looked at one another in shock.

"He thinks that the piece of the Eye is in Sleyne?" Lulath said in Grathian. "But why would the Castle send us here if that were true?"

Even though he wasn't Sleynth, Lulath always spoke of the Castle as though it were a person, with likes and dislikes and motives that humans could understand.

"He's awful," Lilah said in Grathian. "So rude! And you're right, we wouldn't be here if the entire Eye was in Sleyne."

47

She sighed heavily. "We're not getting home anytime soon, are we?"

"Probably not," Rolf agreed, also in Grathian, with his eyes on the wizard. "I was hoping we could con him into handing over the other half of the Eye, and then send us back, but if he doesn't have the Eye—and I believe that part of what he says—then we're probably going home empty-handed."

"I'm not going home empty-handed," Celie argued. "We'll find the piece of the Eye, and then we'll make him send us home."

"Assuming he can," Lulath pointed out. "He is very old, and not very helpful."

The Arkower looked over at them then, and they returned to eating.

Celie gorged herself until she was almost sick, and then she worried that she would do something embarrassing like burp or fall asleep and tumble out of the odd chair she was sitting in. She shook her legs and then started to her feet as Darryn returned. He ran in, face flushed, and tugged at the Arkower's sleeve. The elderly wizard, who really had fallen asleep, grunted at him in irritation and tried to shake him off.

"It's happening," Darryn whispered, but loudly enough that they heard him. "And it's my turn!"

"Excellent," the Arkower said. He got to his feet. "If you will all excuse me, I have some business to attend to. There is a sleeping chamber just there to the left, if you are tired." Then he led Darryn back out through the curtained door.

Celie and the others looked around at one another for a moment.

"What do you think is happening?" Rolf tossed the last hunk of bread to Rufus, who caught it neatly. "And what do you think the Arkower would do if we explored the mountain?"

"I'd like to find out what Darryn meant by it being his turn," Pogue said. He tried to stand, swayed a little, and had to sit down again.

"Be resting, friend Pogue, I will be going," Lulath said. "I am only telling them I shall be looking for a water pot." He grinned at them all and then went to the curtain, listening carefully before parting it to walk through.

And Rufus was right on his heels.

"Rufus, no!" Celie hurried over to grab his harness. Rufus started to croak, and she looked around helplessly.

"Perhaps our bold Rufus is also needing to make the water?" Lulath said with a wink.

Celie grinned back, signaled to the others that it was all right, and she and Lulath went to spy on the Arkower.

Chapter
6

⌒⟐⌒

The corridor that Celie and Lulath found behind the tapestry spiraled down the outer edge of the hollow mountain. It was only dimly lit with lamps, and there were no carpets or moss on the floor at all. Rufus's claws clicked and rasped, and Celie was about to send him back when he stiffened and turned down a little side corridor that she hadn't even seen in the darkness.

"Are you hearing that?" Lulath whispered.

"Yes," Celie whispered back, and they followed Rufus to another curtained doorway.

There was a sound coming from the other side of the curtain. A sound that raised the hairs on Celie's arms and made Rufus hiss. It was a sound that neither of them would ever forget.

Celie pulled Lulath down to her level and whispered directly into his ear. "It's a griffin egg. It's hatching."

"Ah," Lulath breathed.

Rufus lunged through the curtain.

"Rufus, no!"

Celie couldn't help herself. She leaped after her griffin, chasing him into the room where an egg lay in the middle of a pile of blankets. The Arkower, Darryn, and another young man were gathered around it, and they all looked up in shock at Celie and Rufus as they barged into the room.

"Get away," Darryn snapped at them.

Lulath followed Celie. "That is not being of a politeness," he said severely.

"It doesn't matter, just stay clear," the Arkower said, his eyes on the egg in front of them.

It looked exactly like Rufus's egg: as big and orange as a pumpkin. Even from a pace or so away, Celie could feel the heat coming off it. It was rocking back and forth, getting ready to hatch any minute. Rufus was cooing and trying to cuddle the egg, so she grabbed his harness and hauled him away just as the egg tilted and almost stood on one narrow end.

"What an excitement!" Lulath exclaimed. The Arkower shushed him, so the Grathian prince moved closer to Celie, his face eager. "To be seeing a griffin hatch," he said in a quieter voice. "Should I be fetching our friends?"

"No," the Arkower said. "There are too many people here already." He glared at Lulath and Celie.

"And are you to be the rider of this griffin?" Lulath asked Darryn, ignoring the wizard's look. "What the very thrill!"

"Be quiet," Darryn snarled. "He should only know my voice!"

Cracks appeared in the smooth surface of the egg. Celie could hear the little griffin pecking and clawing to break free. Tears started in her eyes as she remembered Rufus's hatching. She'd thought he wouldn't make it, and then he'd almost flown into her arms.

"Oh." She sighed, earning a dirty look from Darryn.

The egg rocked again, and half the shell broke away, revealing a wet, dark gold lion's rump. Then the rest of the shell collapsed, and the newborn griffin shook its bedraggled wings and eagle head free.

"What is this hideous beauty?" Lulath breathed.

The newborn griffin blinked its big golden eyes, looked around, and then made straight toward Lulath. Darryn, an expression of awe on his face, dropped to his knees in front of the little creature and reached for it, but it went right around him with single-minded purpose and threw itself at Lulath's feet.

"Don't touch it, Prince," the Arkower cried. "It's for Darryn!"

Lulath put his hands behind his back, but Celie could see that they were shaking and Lulath's face was filled with longing. The baby griffin was hardly bigger than one of his dogs, and it was crying piteously.

"Then you must be taking care of it with a quickness," Lulath said to Darryn. "It hungers."

"Yes, be quick now," agreed the other young man. He

handed Darryn something that looked like a small cake made out of seeds. "Feed it!"

Darryn waved the cake in front of the griffin's beak, but it just cuddled up to Lulath's shins and wouldn't look at the boy. It was crying even louder now, and Rufus was hovering over it, wings half raised in distress.

"Control your beast," the Arkower snapped as Rufus hissed at Darryn when he tried to shove the cake into the newborn's beak.

"This is awful; they're both upset," Celie told the Arkower. "He doesn't want him!" She pointed at Darryn. "Back away," she urged the boy.

"No, it's my turn!" Darryn sounded near tears.

"You've tried," Celie said, softening. "He's got to eat . . . if he won't take it from you, let Lulath try."

"No!"

Darryn tried to pry open the griffin's beak and force the cake in. The little griffin screamed, and Lulath moved so fast that Celie didn't even see what had happened. All she knew was that suddenly Darryn was halfway across the room, lying on his back with a stunned expression, and Lulath was picking up the newborn griffin and the fallen seed cake. The little griffin took the cake eagerly from Lulath's long fingers and began to munch as Lulath crooned to him in Grathian.

"Is he not the very wonder of wonders?" Lulath said a moment later, in Sleynth. His voice was reverent. "I shall be naming him Lorcan the Destroyer."

"No! It's not fair!" Darryn scrambled to his feet.

"The griffin has chosen," the Arkower intoned, but his face was not pleased.

"It's my turn!" Darryn repeated.

"And you failed," the other young man said sadly. "Again. Just like we all fail, time and again."

He met Celie's eye and gave a grim nod. He held out the basket of seed cakes to her, and she took it, handing them one at a time to Lulath as Lorcan snaffled his way through cake after cake.

"How many eggs have you tried to, um . . . ?" Celie trailed off, unable to think of a word for what she had with Rufus, and now Lulath had with Lorcan.

"Bond?" the young man asked.

"Yes," Celie said.

"I've tried with two eggs; this was Darryn's second." He flicked a glance at the Arkower, and then looked away again.

Celie wondered how many eggs, over how many years, the Arkower had tried to bond with. Tried, and apparently failed.

"I am a wizard," the Arkower said, seeing their looks. "I have no need of a griffin. They are for fighters, not thinkers."

But Celie knew that he was lying. And so did the young man.

"I'm Ethan," he offered.

"Celie."

Her heart was pounding, and she asked the question she couldn't hold back any longer. "What if Darryn had been the only person here?"

"It wouldn't have mattered," Ethan said, and Darryn made a small noise that almost made Celie feel sorry for him. "In the wild his parents would have fed him," Ethan continued. "But since they're . . . gone . . . the griffin would have gotten sick from not eating," Ethan said, and Darryn clenched his fists and turned away. "If they don't like you, they don't like you, and if there's no one that they do like . . ."

"Oh," Celie said. She felt tears in her eyes again. She'd often worried that she was an unfit parent for Rufus, that it was only sheer dumb luck that they had ended up together. But Rufus really had chosen her, and their bond was no accident. If she hadn't been there when he'd hatched . . . she shuddered to think of him alone and sick in the high hatching tower. Another question struck her. "How do you get them to eat once they refuse you?"

"You don't," the Arkower said heavily. "If there isn't an acceptable rider at hand, nor any parents . . . they don't ever eat."

"Oh," Celie said again, feeling sick as he confirmed her suspicions. She looked at him in horror. "How many griffins don't bond with a rider? Is it common?" She frowned around the room. "And how did you bring the egg here? Where are his parents?"

The Arkower silenced Ethan with a chopping motion before the young man could even speak. Darryn looked at

Lulath, looked at the Arkower, and then stormed out of the room.

"We may as well rejoin your companions," the Arkower said, his voice bitter. "I will have more food brought for the beast."

"Darryn's on duty, but I'll bring it," Ethan offered. "He needs to take some time, I'm sure."

Rufus strutted up the corridor to the room where they'd left the others. Celie wasn't sure how much he understood of what had just happened, and how much he'd known was going to happen. Had he sensed the egg, and wanted to go to it? Or had he merely wanted to stretch his legs, and found the egg by accident? And what would have happened if they hadn't arrived? Her heart clenched at the thought.

"Where have you been?" Lilah's face was pasty white with fear when they reached the room again. "We heard noises and . . . oh!" She saw the little griffin and stretched out her hands to stroke it. "Precious!"

"Indeed! Is he not the very precious?" Lulath beamed, holding the baby griffin out for her to admire. "He is being named Lorcan the Destroyer."

Rolf burst out laughing. "I was *not* expecting that," he said. "The name. Or the griffin. Where have you two *been*?"

"We heard a noise down the corridor," Celie began, but the Arkower entered the room behind her and she stopped. She had a feeling that he wouldn't like hearing again about how Darryn had failed to imprint a griffin.

"Yes, yes, now this foreign prince has a griffin," the

Arkower said as though it were of no importance, "and so now we must have a very serious discussion."

They all stopped fussing over Lorcan and gave the wizard their full attention. Celie sank down in a chair, one hand gripping Rufus's harness tightly. Lulath sat on the floor with his new charge, and Ethan slipped in and offered him a platter of food, cut into bite-size pieces. Seeing the look on the Arkower's face and the stillness of the others, Ethan bowed himself back out immediately, though Celie saw a twitch to the tapestry covering the doorway a moment later. She didn't say anything; she could hardly blame him for eavesdropping.

"Now, Prince Lulath of Grath," the Arkower said, "you have an infant griffin. What are you going to do with it?"

They all looked around, communicating as best they could with eyebrows and meaningful looks. Rolf wrinkled his nose at Celie, and Celie grimaced back and made a little motion with one hand at Lulath. Rolf wanted her to do the talking, but he was the Crown Prince and it was Lulath's griffin. Besides, the Arkower frightened her. Lulath was so caught up in feeding Lorcan that he might as well have been back in the Castle for all the attention he paid them.

Rolf sighed and straightened his spine. "We're going to take him back with us to Sleyne, naturally," he said. "Lulath loves animals and will take excellent care of him, just as my sister has taken care of Rufus."

"A fine sentiment, Crown Prince Rolf," the Arkower said. "There is, however, one small problem."

"And what is that?" Celie couldn't help herself.

"I'm afraid that there is no way for you to take these griffins back to Sleyne," the Arkower told them in a tone of gentle regret. "Either of them."

They all sat in shocked silence for a moment.

Lulath was the first to recover. He shook his head at the wizard. "You are telling us the lie," he informed the Arkower. "Rufus is being coming from the Sleyne just this very day of yesterday with us. Why is he not going to his home again? And why is my Lorcan not with him and us?"

"I am certainly not 'telling the lie,' as you so poetically put it, Prince Lulath," the Arkower said. "Once I gladly would have sent you all to Sleyne, children, but no more." He spread out his frail hands, studying the gnarled fingers, and shook his head.

"Come to the point," Rolf said, folding his arms across his chest.

"Princess Cecelia and Prince Lulath just witnessed the problem that has been an even greater plague in our land than the poisoned lake," the Arkower said. "We have few royal griffins left. Whenever people find an egg, they bring it here, and we attempt to bond with it. The young men who serve me take turns in trying . . . and every one of them has failed since the griffins were sent away to Sleyne. We need these bonded griffins here, to show our people how it is done. Apparently we have lost the knack for it, but you have somehow discovered it." He said this as if it pained him.

"There are no griffins, royal or wild, in Sleyne," Celie pointed out. "And that's where the Castle is."

"The Castle is beyond my reach now, and I care nothing for it," the Arkower said, and his words sounded like a lie. "But the griffins, we need the griffins more than the Castle does!"

"You are needing these griffins?" Lulath said in a careful voice. He had stopped feeding Lorcan and was looking at the Arkower with such intensity that it transformed his face, and Celie thought she wouldn't have recognized him if he hadn't been sitting right in front of her. "Whyfor are you needing the griffins, if the Castle does not?"

The Arkower appeared to have noticed the change in the prince as well. "The Castle hardly needs defending," he blustered. "And the griffins are native to this land, not yours. They belong here."

"There is being only one reason that a brain like to mine can see for having a great many young men with a great many griffins, as you are wanting," Lulath said, absently feeding Lorcan with one hand while he continued to gaze with piercing blue eyes at the wizard.

"And what might that be?" The Arkower's voice had an edge like a razor.

"For going to Sleyne and attacking those with no griffins, for bringing the Castle that you love so well back to you and you alone," Lulath said in a voice that was just as sharp. "You are knowing how to go to Sleyne, you are speaking the language in a betterment than I am having, and must have much knowledge of that land. We are not knowing how to get to here, or how to get back from here. You are having griffins, we are not having griffins . . . You are having the lie with us so that you are attacking us."

"Celie," Pogue whispered directly into her ear and she jumped. She hadn't even heard him leave his seat and move over to her. Now he was perched on the arm of her chair, one hand on her elbow to keep her from leaping up.

"What?" Celie tried not to move her lips, after she'd recovered.

"Get on Rufus and go."

"What?"

"Go. Get on Rufus and fly away." He paused. "Lilah, too."

"This is nonsense," the Arkower was saying to Lulath in a level voice.

"Then let us be coming and going with freedom," Lulath retorted.

"Go now," Pogue whispered again.

"No, I—"

Pogue seized her around the waist and whipped her off her chair and onto Rufus's back before she could finish her protest. Then he had hold of Lilah, and Lilah leaped behind Celie with little urging.

"What are you doing?" The Arkower half rose from his seat in alarm.

"Be going," Lulath shouted. "We can be finding you later!"

"Stop them," the Arkower said, hardly raising his voice.

Ethan and Darryn burst into the room, along with another man Celie had never seen before. She grabbed the handles of Rufus's harness.

Rufus took off.

Celie was amazed that Rufus could understand the underlying menace in the Arkower's words. That, or he just wanted to be away from the Arkower as desperately as Celie did. He ran right around the startled Ethan, heading to the edge of the long spiraling ramp that had brought them to the Arkower's chambers.

Extending his wings, he plunged over the edge. Celie screamed, though she knew he had plenty of room to fly, and tried to get a better grip on the harness. Lilah grabbed Celie's waist painfully tight and buried her face in Celie's hair. Celie recovered quickly and pushed the handles forward, urging Rufus to go down to the entrance. But Rufus circled and then began to fly upward, toward the hollow peak of the mountain.

"Where are you going?" Celie called to him, and he screeched in reply.

Then, just above the Arkower's living quarters, she saw it: a broad, jagged hole in the side of the mountain. It was large enough for a full-grown griffin to pass through without pulling in his wings, and Rufus was only half-grown. They sailed through and out into the open air, where another griffin waited for them.

It was Rufus's father. He gave a cry of greeting and turned to fly alongside them.

"Are you coming?" Celie called to him. "Let's go that way!"

And she pointed both griffins toward the ruins of the Castle.

Chapter 7

Celie had never flown with Rufus for such a great distance, and with such speed. It was exhilarating, though it also made her sad that her poor griffin hadn't been able to really stretch his wings before now. It comforted her to think that if they returned to Sleyne, since everyone at the Castle knew about him now, he would no longer be a secret. He could fly as much as he liked, and in daylight, too.

When they returned to Sleyne. When. Celie said this to herself several times to make it feel truer.

But she soon found it was also rather tiring to hold on to a speeding griffin for very long. Minutes of flying, which Celie was used to, stretched into an hour, which she was not. She began swaying in her seat, eyes fluttering closed, as nerves and lack of sleep caught up to her. Fortunately Rufus, sensing her inattention, would scream loudly whenever she was just about to drift off, and she would jerk herself upright again.

She and Lilah tried to talk, but the wind carried their words away. Also, the only thing they had to say to each other was that they would return for the others soon and go home to Sleyne. Soon.

The sun had set as they reached the far shore, and they soared over the edge of the forest. Lilah tugged at Celie's waist and pointed over her shoulder.

"We can't go back without them," she shouted into Celie's ear.

"It's too dark," Celie called back, and her teeth began to chatter with cold. "We'll wait in the tower for morning."

Flying was always cold, courtesy of the wind and one's proximity to the clouds, and she had no cloak. In addition to that, her gown had several rips in it, from catching on the grabbing branches of the forest, and the wind was slicing right through every one of them.

"I don't know how you stand it," Lilah said, her teeth chattering. "I'm freezing! Did you really fly around the Castle at night?"

"Yes," Celie said, thinking of how easy things had been when keeping Rufus a secret was her biggest worry. "We're going to have to have a warm place to sleep," she said, and Rufus tilted his head to show that he had heard her. "Head for the tower."

Rufus's father was still flying alongside Rufus, and Celie wished that there was some way she could send him back to fetch her companions. Rufus would understand if she asked him to go back for Rolf and the others, and she wished that she dared send him, but she could tell that he was tiring, and she knew she wouldn't ask him to fly all that way again.

But before they reached the ruins, and as Rufus started to fly lower over the trees from exhaustion, the other griffin squawked and veered to the right. Rufus started to follow him, and Celie panicked and yanked on the harness, digging her heels into his sides as well to try to keep him on course. If they landed too far into the forest they'd be hopelessly lost.

But Rufus's father flew ahead of them and cried out again even louder. His call was commanding, and Celie knew that she had lost. Rufus's whole attention was on the larger griffin now, and she had no choice but to hang on.

They swerved again to the right and then Rufus's father began to descend. Celie refreshed her grip on the harness as Rufus also began to go down among the trees, landing in a sandy clearing to the west of the lake.

"Now what?" Lilah asked, releasing her painful grip on Celie's waist.

"I suppose we might as well get some rest," Celie said doubtfully. "It's too dark to go back for the others."

Neither of them knew how to make a fire, but Lilah made a hollow in the sand and they curled up together. Rufus lay down next to Celie, radiating warmth, and after a moment, his father lay down beside Lilah. She made a small *eep*, but when he just sighed and appeared to go to sleep, she relaxed.

Celie wasn't sure she would be able to sleep, with everything that had happened. She wiggled away from Lilah just a little, so that she could pull Rufus the lion out of her bodice and give him a secret cuddle.

"What is it?" Lilah asked drowsily. "What are you doing?"

"I—I found this in the griffin stable," Celie told her, rolling over so that Lilah could see her stuffed lion in the moonlight.

"It's Rufus," Lilah said in astonishment.

Celie's griffin raised his head and made a questioning noise.

"Not you, Rufus, but that Rufus," Lilah said, reaching out to touch the toy. "*Where* did you say you found him?"

"In the griffin stable, just before the Arkower came," Celie said. "Rufus's parents had him all along. Because—" She stopped. It felt strange to say it aloud. "Because Rufus's father is the one who ate Khelsh," she said finally.

"Is he really?" Lilah sounded impressed. She reached behind her back and thumped Rufus's father's side. "Good job, sir!"

Rufus's father lifted his head, gazing down at Lilah in the moonlight. Her eyes were starting to close from exhaustion, though, and she didn't seem to notice.

"I hope Khelsh was a tasty meal," she said sleepily. "The Arkower looks a little stringy, though . . ."

"Lilah," Celie said, startled. "Don't tell him to eat the Arkower!"

"If the Arkower's not going to send us home, what good is he?" Lilah countered, her eyes shut.

"He's . . . he's . . . he really isn't any help, I suppose." Celie sighed.

She wanted to talk to Lilah some more, but Lilah was asleep now. She wanted to plan how they would get the others free, get the missing piece of the Eye, and get home, too. But soon she was spiraling down to sleep, a warm griffin pressed against her back.

✦ ✦ ✦

"Wake up, Cel!"

The next thing she knew, it was dawn—and Rolf was standing over her.

"Rolf!" She staggered to her feet. "You made it out!"

She blinked around and saw Lilah hugging Pogue and then Lulath, her cheeks flushed. Celie quickly hugged Rolf and then Pogue, who was looking much better, and Lulath, who had his baby griffin stuck in the front of his tunic. He pointed to the stuffed lion sticking out of her bodice, and they shared a smile.

Standing to one side of the clearing, looking awkward, was Ethan.

"How did you all get out?" Lilah asked.

"It was being this Ethan," Lulath said.

"It was Prince Lulath's doing," Ethan said at the same time.

"We brought food," Rolf offered a beat later. "While you hear our tale of adventure."

They sat down and he handed around bread and cheese from a bag.

"Don't forget to steal food for your escape, I always say," Rolf told them cheerfully.

"How often do you escape from places?" Pogue asked, amused.

"More often than I'd like," Rolf countered, handing him a wedge of cheese.

Pogue took his portion and ate with better appetite than he'd shown the day before. He noticed Celie watching and raised his eyebrows. She blushed and looked away, concentrating on her own food.

"So, we are being told by this Arkower that we are not leaving, not ever," Lulath began. "And you taking the leave, with much shouting."

"I think he wanted to use me and Pogue as ransom to get you and Rufus back, Cel," Rolf interrupted.

"Precise," Lulath agreed. "So I am making very much fuss, that my Lorcan he is sickening. He must be having a certain food, I am a raiser of the sort of dogs, and do know what tiny animals are needing, and so much so forth."

"It was a sight to behold," Rolf said, his eyes shining. "He was leaping around the room, waving his arms and flinging poor Lorcan around until I thought he really would be sick!"

"It was not my favorite thing that I have been doing," Lulath said. He stroked the griffin head that poked out of the elaborate lacings of his tunic. "But it was being of a necessary!"

"Then what happened?" Lilah asked. She looked around. "Are you sure you weren't followed?"

"We have a little time," Ethan told her, "but we should move along soon."

"To where?" Lilah wanted to know.

"Let them tell the story first," Celie said, exasperated.

"So, to be quickly going," Lulath said, "I am making the insistence that the Arkower of himself is bringing me certain food, and so much forth. Or having it broughten, to say. And when he is leaving, we are going down and around, to get out of this terrible mountain, and we are finding Ethan!"

"I told them they were going the long way," Ethan supplied, as though eager to prove to Celie and Lilah that he could be trusted. "I took them out one of the side tunnels and down one of the more hidden trails."

"I see," Lilah said, lips pursed. She studied Ethan closely. "Now tell me, how is it that you speak Sleynth?"

"We all learn Sleynth as part of serving the Arkower," Ethan said. He nodded at Lulath. "The prince is right. He's never said it, but I believe that the Arkower plans to take over your country. He wants the Castle and the griffins, even after all this time."

Lilah arranged her dirty skirts around her knees. Celie

braced herself, and saw Rolf sit up straighter as well. Lilah looked perfectly at ease, but her sister and brother knew she was about to go on the attack.

"We should probably be on our way soon," Lilah said as though commenting on the weather.

As though a wizard weren't searching for them.

"But before we do, I have a few questions for you," Lilah went on, and she fixed her gaze on Ethan, who was intelligent enough to squirm despite her still-casual air. "Questions like, why is the Arkower preparing for attack now, when he's had hundreds of years?"

"He—he—" Ethan stammered.

"How many of you are there, and how is he planning to attack?"

"We—there are only—"

"You're not taking another step with us, no matter how much you helped with the escape from the mountain last night, until I get satisfactory answers," Lilah said pleasantly. She arched an eyebrow. *"Do you understand?"* She finished in a menacing tone that made Celie shift away from her.

"Oooh," Rolf said, eyes gleaming.

Ethan looked around for support, but they all just looked back. Celie was holding her breath. Would Ethan tell them? Could he help them? Or was he really a spy?

The boy ducked his head, his ears and cheeks flaming. "I'll tell you everything I know," he mumbled. "I swear. But I don't really know all of it. I mean, I was told when I was eight that I would go to the mountain and serve the

Arkower. My parents are dead; I didn't have another choice. The older boys, the ones before me, they find ways to leave. To sneak away . . . They are ashamed when they realize that no matter how badly they want a griffin, the griffins don't want them."

Lilah made an impatient gesture, and Ethan hurried to continue.

"I think the Arkower originally wanted to build up the Glorious Arkower again. We had parts of the Castle, and there were some griffins left. But no one has ever bonded with one of the griffins, and they don't breed as quickly as they used to."

"Because the Castle is gone? Or is there another reason?" Celie asked.

Ethan shrugged. "I don't know. He gave up his name and became the Arkower, as though he was dead and our land was dead. But I think he had a vision of restoring our land, our griffins, our Castle." He licked his lips nervously. "It was ours first, you know."

"We know," Rolf said, circling his hand to encourage Ethan to keep going.

"But that didn't work, so . . ." Ethan shrugged.

"So now he's going after our griffins and our Castle?" Celie asked, but she didn't need to. Ethan nodded. "How?"

"I really don't . . . well, he wanted to use the shard of the Eye that's still here, but it got stolen. That's how I found out about his plan to go to Sleyne."

"So he needs the Eye to travel to Sleyne?" Pogue asked,

looking thoughtful. "I wonder if we could use it to get home without his help, then."

"I don't know," Ethan said.

"Where is the shard of the Eye?" Lilah asked.

"I don't know that, either," Ethan said. "If I knew . . . well, I would have told the Arkower." He made a face. "It's difficult to keep secrets from a wizard."

"That is being the truth," Lulath said. "Even the Bran, who is kind, is making me to want to confess when I have nothing to confess."

"Who stole the shard?" Celie asked.

Ethan looked around at Rufus and his father. "This is going to sound very odd, and I did try to tell the Arkower, who didn't believe me. I swear it was a griffin." He lowered his voice. "That griffin." He pointed to Rufus's father, hastily dropping his hand when he saw the griffin looking back.

They all stared at the big golden griffin. He preened his feathers, and Celie startled them all with a burst of laughter. She believed Ethan. It was exactly the kind of thing that Rufus would have done: steal a shiny gem like the Eye. And now they had a better chance of finding it! There was every possibility that Rufus's father could lead them right to it!

"Who does the Arkower think stole it?" Lilah asked.

"The Treaty-breaker," Ethan said.

"Who?"

Ethan squirmed. "That's what we are supposed to call

him. He's the old Royal Wizard and the last Hathelocke." He tilted his head at Celie. "Well, until you came here."

"I'm not a Hathelocke," Celie said in frustration. "I'm a Glower!"

"Well, technically we're Hathelocke on our mother's side. And Arkower on our father's," Rolf pointed out.

"Arkish," Ethan corrected him.

"Yes, Arkish," Rolf said with a nod. "Our father's family is Arkish, and our mother's is Hathelocke. So, I suppose you could call us Arklockes." He paused. "No, don't. That sounds awful."

"This treaty-breaker, he's the old Royal Wizard?" Pogue said, ignoring Rolf. He frowned. "But I thought the Arkower was."

"The Arkower was the greatest Arkish wizard," Ethan said. "And the broker of the peace between us and the Hathelockes. But the Treaty-breaker . . . I don't know his real name," he confessed, "he was the Royal Wizard of the Castle."

"I—wait—you're just going to have to tell us more," Rolf said.

"But not here," Pogue said. "We've stayed here too long. We need to get moving." He stood up and looked toward the lake. "Should we just keep going along the shore?"

"It is being best if we are to stay within the covering trees, Friend Pogue," Lulath said. He stood up and brushed the sand off his clothes, which were much the worse for wear. "If only there was being another place to be resting, that is not the Castle. For surety the Arkower is seeking us there, and there he is finding us simply."

Rolf helped Lilah and Celie to their feet, and the girls dusted each other off. Their gowns were so creased and stained that they were probably ruined. Of course, if they didn't get home, it would hardly matter.

"I wonder what the other thing on the map is?" Celie said, gazing at Lilah's cape.

"What map?" Pogue followed Celie's gaze. He frowned. "I don't—"

"What in the name of—there's a map of the Glorious Arkower on Lilah's back!" Rolf exclaimed. "It looks just like the wooden one back at the Castle!"

"Yes!" Celie clutched at Rolf's arm, pointing to the map with her other hand. "Do you see it, too? I noticed it before on the boat but didn't want to say anything in front of the Arkower."

"May I be seeing?" Lulath went eagerly behind Lilah to look as well. "A wonder!" he cried. He pointed to the lake and the mountains. "Here is being the Arkower's only home, and here is being the Castle." He pointed to the pillar shape at the bottom of the map, while Lilah strained her head over her shoulder to see what they were looking at. "But yes, what is this being?" He rested his finger on the other pillar. "It is not being far from here."

Pogue waved to Ethan, summoning him. "You must know," he said bluntly.

"I shouldn't tell you," Ethan said.

"Now you have to," Rolf told him, his face severe. "We need all the information we can get!"

"All right," Ethan said, his face chalky. "I shouldn't, but . . . it's . . . it's the Tomb of the Builder."

"The Builder?" Celie's heart started to pound.

"I want . . . I hoped to go with you to the Castle," Ethan went on. "In Sleyne. But not if you're going in there first," he babbled.

"A tomb? Is it haunted?" Rolf looked delighted.

"It's the Tomb of the *Builder*," Ethan repeated.

"The Builder of the Castle?" Celie swallowed, trying to calm herself. "There's a tomb and it's big enough to be on the map?" She exchanged excited looks with the others.

"Hollowing out that mountain was no mean feat," Pogue said. "He must have been a great man, and powerful."

"He didn't do it himself," Lilah pointed out. "I'm sure he had lots of people working for him."

"But he designed the Castle," Celie said. "He was in charge?"

"Yes," Ethan said. "And he was a very great man. We shouldn't disturb his rest. He . . . you shouldn't disturb his rest." His face twisted. "The Arkower made me steal something from it . . . Darryn, too. That's why the griffins didn't want us. They know."

"That is being nonsense!" Lulath slapped him on the back and nearly knocked him down. "The griffins, they are not being such . . . and how are they knowing?"

"We need to move now," Pogue said. "We've stood around here too long." He paused. "What did you steal from the tomb?"

"But we're going to the Tomb of the Builder, right?" Rolf asked. "You could put back whatever it was you stole, Ethan. Because we're going there right now!"

"I can't," Ethan protested. "It's gone!"

"That doesn't matter," Celie said. "But we've come all this way, and lived in the Castle all our lives, and we never even knew there *was* a Builder," she said to Ethan by way of apology. "We can't leave without at least taking a look."

Chapter
8

I don't like this," Lilah announced.

"It's just making you nervous because we're all staring at your back," Rolf assured her. "Which is just as lovely as ever. Also, your hair is remarkably shiny despite everything we've been through."

Pogue laughed softly and Lilah continued to grumble. Celie just kept plodding along beside Rufus, who kept looking up with envy at his father, swooping and wheeling high above them. She was keeping him on a short lead because Rufus showed every inclination of heading back to drink out of the lake whenever Celie let go of him, and he was too tired from yesterday's flying for her to ride. So they were forced to walk through the forest, with Rufus straining against his harness, searching for the tomb.

"It is not being the best of maps, this Lilah cape," Lulath said to Celie, trying to cheer her up. "But it is being the best of maps that we are having. And how bright of your brain to see it as a map!"

"Thank you," Celie said. "It is a bit too regular, though, isn't it? I mean, to make the fabric look better. Nothing's really that round." She pointed to the circle of lake.

"Oh, but it is being the very rounded," Lulath said. "And so is the valley in which the Castle is now sitting. I am thinking it is being made in this fashion."

"I guess the Castle likes being at the bottom of a bowl," Celie agreed. "And if the Builder could hollow out the mountains and make the outside so smooth, I suppose he could make the lake rounder."

"Perhaps it is making it feel the safety, this bowl," Lulath said. "But the army that comes down from the mountains would be having the better part."

"Really?"

"Oh, yes!" Lulath told her. "They are winning the battles, mostly always, the armies on the highest ground." He laughed. "That is being my other passion, the military strategying."

"It is?" She stared at him. She'd never heard this before.

"Yes," Lulath said. "Since I am the smallest of boys I am in love with two things: the making of wars and the training of the small dogs!" He laughed, and then began to whistle.

Celie reflected that Lulath was somehow the happiest, strangest, and most interesting person she knew, all at the same time.

"So," she said a minute later. "Do you think you could

negotiate with the Arkower? To make him send us all home, with the Eye? And Lorcan?"

"Oh, surely!" He nodded his head several times. "That is why I am having a liking of your family so very, very, my Celie! When I am coming to Sleyne I am thinking that it is but your father who is a very man, with his mighty Castle. But then I am having the acquaintances of yourself, our Rolf, our Lilah, and our others, and I am thinking, here are the people like you, Lulath!"

"Like you?"

"The people who wonder at the world, and make it to be very better and mighty."

"Oh," Celie said.

"We are all strong friends," Lulath said. "Together and apart. We will be getting home with honors."

"I hope so," Celie said.

"Oh, but a surety, our Celie!" Lulath looked at her in concern. "Do you not believe your Lulath?"

"I—I want to," Celie said. "But it just seems so hopeless." She lowered her voice. "And I—I'm so afraid. How can you never be afraid of anything?"

"Me? Not being afraid?" Lulath threw back his head and laughed. Everyone turned to look at him, but he just kept laughing, and after a minute they kept plodding along. "I am knowing so many fears, our Celie!" he said at last.

"You are?"

"Oh, so many! In the bad times, when that Khelsh did control the Castle? It was a terrible fear that had me!"

Celie gaped at him. "But you just walked all over the Castle, whenever you wanted! You brought me things, you were . . . you were afraid?"

"Oh, so much fear," Lulath said. "But then I would look to myself in the mirror and say, Lulath, you silly big man! Here is being two beautiful princess and a noble prince in so much the danger! Have they food? Have they warmth? You must be putting on your shoes like a very man, and going forth! And so I am!" He nodded firmly. "It is why also I am studying the strategying when I am young. I am having so much the fear in the night, I think, I will learn all that is brave and very, and will also go forth with strongness!"

Pogue, who had been behind them, walking closer and closer until he was almost on Celie's heels, leaned forward then. "Lulath, that is the most astonishing thing you've ever said. You continue to surprise me."

"I thank you, friend Pogue," Lulath said cheerfully. "It is because I am looking such a silly man. I am liking the clothes too much, it is a thing that I know. You are not thinking that I am having much brain."

"I . . . didn't say that," Pogue said, his cheeks faintly red.

"Oh, but you are thinking it, and it is not a bother," Lulath said. "So many are thinking it of this silly prince!" He fished in his pocket and brought out a hard lump of cheese, which he broke into pieces for Lorcan, whistling as he fed the little griffin.

"My," Celie said in a low voice to Pogue. "Goodness."

"I'm not sure whether I'm more impressed, or more guilty," Pogue said under his breath. "I did indeed think of him as a 'silly big man' . . ."

"It's the dogs," Celie said. "And the lace."

"So much lace," Pogue agreed.

"We're here," Rolf announced. From behind him Ethan made a faint strangled noise.

They were in a small clearing, and before them rose a great mound, the Tomb of the Builder. The earthy dome, overgrown by scrubby little plants and tough grass, completely filled the little clearing. The tomb was perfectly round, stretching out to either side like a giant's porridge bowl turned upside down.

Rufus's father landed nearby and carked at Rufus. Celie let go of her griffin's harness and he went to his sire while Celie shook out her hand, which had gone numb from gripping the harness so tightly.

"Stay here," Celie told Rufus firmly. "There isn't room for you inside."

Rufus bobbed his head and he and his father began grooming each other, unconcerned about the tomb or the rill of excitement that had just run through the humans. Lulath gave them each some of the bread from his pocket, and some to Lorcan.

"You see," Rolf said to Ethan. "The griffins don't mind that we're here."

"I don't see a door," Lilah said. "How do we get in?"

"It's over there," Ethan told her reluctantly. "If you must go inside, can I stay out here?"

"Suit yourself," Rolf said. He was already walking around to the far side of the tomb.

Everyone but Ethan followed Rolf, anxious and excited by turns. Celie could see the two emotions warring in Lilah's face as she walked beside her sister. She grabbed Lilah's elbow and gave it a little squeeze, as much to reassure herself as Lilah.

"The Tomb of the Builder," Celie whispered.

"This could be a very bad idea," Lilah whispered back.

Celie disagreed, silently. They were going to see the tomb of the man who had built the Castle! What wonders would they find there? What answers to her many questions?

But, at the same time, it was a *tomb*. There was a dead man inside, and Celie wouldn't want to disrespect anyone's final resting place . . . particularly not someone who had created her beloved Castle!

"Here," Pogue said. "The door's on the north side, of course."

"What do you mean, of course?" Lilah asked.

"All tombs face north," Pogue said. "North is the top of the world, closest to the heavens."

"In Grath we are facing east, to the seas," Lulath said, but more like he was making conversation than arguing, and he was the first to follow Pogue around to the north side of the mound.

"I've read that," Pogue said. "But in the ancient tombs of Sleyne, it's always north."

"And Sleyne *is* coming from the Arkower," Lulath agreed.

"I'm not sure I want to be associated with these people," Lilah sniffed as she, Celie, and Rolf followed them.

"Don't worry," Rolf told her. "Remember, we're also descended from their mortal enemies, the Hathelockes!"

"Stop saying that," Lilah retorted. "It's making me feel funny."

Celie felt funny, too. But it was more like an itching in her palms and a twitching in her muscles that made her want to go inside the tomb, rather than any sort of gloom and doom about their long-dead ancestors.

"Over here," Pogue called.

On the north side of the mound was a large dent about Lilah's height. It was covered by a hanging curtain of ferns, but as Pogue lifted the greenery away a thick wooden door was revealed.

"Here we go," Pogue said, sounding almost as excited as Rolf.

Lulath tucked Lorcan more securely into his tunic and he and Pogue began to tear at the ferns, which kept falling down on them. Rolf danced from foot to foot for a moment, then finally let out a curse and joined the others in uncovering the door. After that there was the latch to contend with, a large iron contraption that appeared to have no key and wouldn't move. Rolf lifted his leg high and kicked it a few times.

Lilah made an irritated noise, rolling her eyes at Celie.

"I can feel you rolling your eyes, Delilah," Rolf said over his shoulder. "You could go and get Ethan, if you want to help."

"Oh, no, carry on," she said airily. "I wouldn't want to ruin your fun."

"I am having it!" Lulath cried out. He was grasping the loop of iron in both hands. "It is contrary to our closings!"

He heaved back, twisting the latch to the right at the same time, face tense. Pogue put his hands next to Lulath's and twisted, too. There was a horrible groaning and scraping noise, and Pogue made a drawn-out yell as they very slowly moved backward. Then it all gave way with a lurch, the door sprang open, and Lulath and Pogue fell against Rolf. All three of them landed on the ground, and Lilah leaped out of the way just in time to avoid Lulath's crushing her.

A broad, low door hung open in front of them. Beyond it was nothing but darkness.

"I am so much the elation," Lulath said in a hushed voice.

"Me, too," whispered Celie.

Chapter 9

Pogue went to the entrance and tentatively stuck his head inside and looked around. He pulled back and they all watched anxiously as he breathed in and out and finally spoke.

"It's dark but seems safe enough, though the air's a little stale," he announced.

"Let's go, then," Rolf said. "I can deal with stale air."

"So can I," Celie said, grabbing the back of Rolf's tunic so that she was right behind him.

Pogue stepped aside and let them go in first, although his expression was wary. He followed close behind, with Lilah on his heels and Lulath on hers.

There were four stone steps going down, and then they were standing on a smooth stone floor. There was a sense of space around them, but also Celie could feel things crowding that space. Ethan had told them that there were torches and a tinderbox near the last step, so Pogue and Rolf fumbled around for a minute, then finally located and lit a pair of torches.

The light flared, and Lilah screamed.

"What is it?" Rolf brandished his torch, and let out a yell, too. There was a man standing only a pace away from them.

Celie's knees turned to water and her throat seized up. She tried to back slowly out of the tomb but couldn't move more than an inch.

"Oh," Lulath cried out after a terrifying minute, "it is being armor! It is being the king's only armor." He laughed, lighting a torch of his own and moving closer to illuminate the suit of armor, arranged on a rack so that it looked alive. "Fine work, of the bronze," he noted. "Ah!"

He leaned around the armor and touched his torch to something. It was another torch, which sputtered and then came to life. Pogue moved to the other side of the door and found two more torches in sconces and lit them. Slowly the shadows in the mound lifted, and Celie felt her heart lifting with them, like Rufus taking flight.

The Tomb of the Builder.

"Look at the helmet," Celie breathed to Rolf, pointing a shaking finger at the armor.

It was shaped like a griffin's head, with the beak curving down to form the nose guard. The griffin's "eyes" were huge topazes the size of Celie's palm, that glittered in the torchlight and seemed to be following them as they crept farther inside.

Lulath found more torches and lit them, and soon the domed tomb was bathed in flickering golden light.

"Oh. My." Lilah clapped her hands lightly. "Oh. My. Goodness."

It was a treasure trove, like something from a story. A hoard worthy of a dragon, or the lair of some fabled thief. It was all cobweb covered, grimy, and stale, but Celie had never seen such riches in her life.

There were bushel baskets of gold coins, open chests of jewelry, and bolts of fabric that gleamed with silver and gold bullion embroidery beneath a layer of dust. There were racks of weapons and statues of women and children that had been painted to make them appear more lifelike. They wore clothing, too, of rich velvets and silk, and the women wore real crowns and necklaces of ruby and emerald and opal.

"Ah!" Lulath found a holder for his torch and stuck it in. This freed up his hands to wave around at the statues and weapons. "Ah! I am doing reading of this! He is being buried with all the splendor! With the family and the things that are his!"

"The family? But they're just statues," Celie said.

She reached out and delicately touched the folds of the nearest statue's gown. It was dusty, but underneath the dust the satin was still a shining violet color. The statue itself was of a tall woman with a proud face, looking into the distance with eyes that had been painted blue. She had brown-painted hair, wore a crown of sapphires and pearls, and was more handsome than beautiful, with a rather long nose. There were two smaller statues on each side of her, both of young girls, wearing necklaces of rubies and gowns of straw-colored silk.

"They are being statues of the wives and the children, because they are not being dead, most probably," Lulath explained. "Or they are being buried in another place. The wife is being buried in the home of her people, instead of in this place, in the perhaps."

Lulath pointed to another of the adult-size statues. This was of a curvaceous woman of medium height, and her skin had been painted a mahogany color. Her hair had been carved as intricately coiled braids, and she wore a crown of strange workmanship that looked like a pair of snakes wrapped around her brow. The snakes had winking pale-green gems for eyes that matched the clasps on her gown, which was of sheer white fabric that had been wound around her form and fastened at the shoulders. There were four child-size statues around her of three boys and a girl, all with skin painted several shades lighter, but with the same black hair in intricate braids.

"This is the greatest thing we have ever done," Rolf announced. He was bouncing on the balls of his feet, turning in circles to take it all in. "Can you imagine? No one has seen these things for thousands of years! We don't even have words for these weapons! Or names for these people or where they're from!"

"How many wives did he *have?*" Lilah asked. "There are *five* women here!"

"I would guess five, then," Pogue said in a dry voice.

"And nineteen children," Lilah said, counting them. She threw up her hands. "No wonder the Castle has so many bedrooms!"

Celie laughed, giddy.

"It is such an amazement, that he is having five queens," Lulath said. "I would not have been thinking it! But marvelous!"

"I would never marry anyone who had more than one wife," Lilah said, horrified.

"Oh, it is not being bad," Lulath told her with a shrug. "We are sometimes having the many wives in the history of my Grath. Many of wives, they are being as great friends as can be seen."

Lilah gave him a narrow look. "How many wives do you plan on having?"

Lulath's face turned bright red. He spread out his hands and gave her an innocent look. "Am I to think of such things? Now?" he said.

Before Lilah could reply, Rolf interrupted.

"All right, enough of that," Rolf said. "Have a little respect for the dead, who do not need to hear you flirting!"

"What dead?" Lilah asked, hiding her red cheeks with her hands. "These are statues."

"There's even his dogs," Pogue said, loudly. Looking

over, Celie thought that Pogue looked a little red as well, and he stepped over a basket of coins with unnecessary stomping of his boots.

Opposite the wives and children were ranks of statues of dogs and even something that looked like a kind of wild-cat. They all wore tooled leather collars, and one of the larger dogs had a sort of harness across its back, bearing two quivers of arrows. The floor was so crowded that it was impossible to walk. Celie moved past a basket containing bottles of wine to have a closer look at the dogs, and ended up walking around a tapestry that was hanging from the ceiling at the back of the tomb.

"The pets are even more bizarre than the statues of the children," Lilah said.

Her voice sounded muffled by the thick cloth curtain-ing off the part of the tomb where Celie was now standing, rooted to the spot. She took another small step forward, then stopped again.

"It's not bizarre," Rolf argued. "It's impressive. Look how rich he was! Look at how much stuff he had!"

"See, that's what's so awful," Lilah said. "You're basically saying this dead king was vain and wanted everyone to know how much he had, but who would see it? Grave robbers?"

"You're missing the point," Pogue said. "You can't actu-ally take your gold with you to heaven, but there are people who believe that if you have it buried with you, you can at least prove that you were important."

"And that's supposed to matter?" Lilah asked. "What if he was some kind of monster, and everyone hated him, but he's rich so he gets to go to heaven?"

"Yes, but at the same time, you're missing the point," Pogue said impatiently.

Celie had never heard him talk this way to Lilah before. She wanted to see his face, but she didn't dare to move another step.

"It's not so much that he's buying his way in," Pogue went on, "it's that he's showing what he *accomplished*. It's completely different!"

"You're talking like you know him," Lilah said with irritation. "And he's not only long dead, his body isn't even here! This isn't really a tomb: it's just a greedy man's way of hiding his things from the world!"

"No," Celie said. The word came out as a little choking noise, so she cleared her throat and tried again. "No, he's here," she said.

"What was that?" Pogue called to her. "Celie? Where are you?"

"Celie!" There was a rustling sound as Lilah looked for her. "Where did you go?"

"Over . . . over here," Celie said. "With him."

Pogue ducked around the tapestry dividing the tomb, his belt knife drawn. He looked at Celie to make sure she was all right, and she just pointed to what she'd found. The others followed Pogue, their continued chatter breaking off suddenly.

"And here is the very king," Lulath exclaimed, not one to be silenced for long. "How wondrous!"

Lulath was right. It was the very king. The king who had built the Castle, lying on a narrow marble bed in a robe of purple velvet, wearing a crown that looked like the top of one of the Castle's towers made of jewel-encrusted gold. He had his hands folded on his chest, just over the hilt of his broadsword.

And he was very dead.

And so was the griffin lying on the adjoining marble bed. A bier, Celie remembered suddenly. It was called a bier.

"That's disgusting," Lilah squawked.

"It's their *tomb*," Rolf pointed out. "Where did you think they would be?"

"Well they . . . oh!" Lilah just threw up her hands, and then put an arm around Celie. "Are you all right?"

"Yes," Celie said.

She was, oddly enough. Now that she'd gotten over the initial shock, she was very much all right. They didn't look decayed. Much like the fabrics and goods on the other side of the tapestry, or the tools and cloth that had appeared over the years in the Castle, there was no sign of the years that had passed . . . but they were nevertheless dead. The king's face was stiff and dry and the griffin looked fragile, like an old butterfly cocoon.

"The master of the very Castle," Lulath said with reverence. "He is being perhaps the most very man of every century and land!"

"And a griffin rider," Celie said. The griffin's beak was almost touching the king's shoulder, and Celie had the sudden urge to try and scoot them closer together.

"He created the Castle," Pogue said with great respect. "This man."

"And he had nineteen children and five wives," Rolf said. "Which is almost as great an accomplishment, at least in my view."

Celie ignored Rolf. She was looking at the rings on the king's sunken fingers. There were two plain gold rings, set with emeralds, on his right hand, but on his left was a ring shaped like a castle turret, much like his crown. The color of the gold and the workmanship looked breathtakingly familiar. She leaned over and studied the ring from a better angle.

"Careful!" Lilah grabbed her arm and pulled her back. "Don't touch him!"

"It's not like you can catch death from a thousand-year-old body," Rolf argued as Celie gave the ring another look, ignoring Lilah's insistent tugging.

There was something about the ring that drew her eye. She felt as if she knew this ring, as though she had seen it before, many times, but almost forgotten it. Her feet and hands itched a little, and she rubbed her palms absently against her grimy skirt.

"This is the mate to Daddy's ring," she announced, cutting off Rolf and Lilah's argument over whether it was disrespectful to lean over the body of a king. "The griffin ring."

"What? No," Rolf said slowly, leaning over beside Celie. "I mean, look at it. It's nothing like Father's ring."

Celie just shook her head at him. She was certain of it.

"I think Celie's right," Lilah said, her voice pinched as though she were trying not to breathe too deeply near the dead king. "It's exactly like Father's."

"I don't see what you're talking about," Rolf said again. "And I've *worn* the griffin ring, remember?"

"No, Celie's right," Pogue said. He was tall enough that he could stand behind Lilah and still lean over enough to see the ring. He nodded his head, his hair flopping over the fading bruises on his temple. "It's the same craftsmanship. Same weight, too, and the same gems and gold alloy."

"See! And Pogue knows these things," Lilah said.

"*Now* you listen to me," Pogue muttered.

"And there is being the marks of the other ring," Lulath said.

He pointed a long finger to the king's right hand. There were the two plain rings with their beautifully cut gems, on the king's first and third fingers, but on the middle finger was a deep depression where a ring had been. Now that Celie was looking for it, she could see the pattern of the wings and beak of her father's ring marking the dead king's finger.

"The ring of the first king of Castle Glower," Lilah said in awe.

"I wonder how much better Father could control the Castle, with both rings," Rolf said.

"No one can control the Castle," Celie objected.

"Poor choice of words," Rolf conceded. "I wonder how much better Father could *communicate* with the Castle, if he had the other ring?"

Celie had to agree with this. It was very possible that with two rings the Castle would obey the king, as much as it pained her to think of the Castle's being at anyone's beck and call, even her father's.

"Pogue, are you thinking of the crown, too? As I am seeing the crown, it is giving me wonderings," Lulath said.

"Let me have a look," Pogue said.

He moved around Celie and stood at the head of the bier, his hands behind his back to avoid touching anything. He studied the crown closely for a moment and then nodded and looked up at them.

"I'd bet my life the crown and both rings were forged by the same goldsmith, from the same materials," Pogue said.

"What does that mean?" Lilah wanted to know. "I mean, I know what that *means*, but what does it mean for *Father*?"

"It might mean nothing," Pogue said with a shrug. "But it might be the key to understanding the Castle."

"What do we do?" Lilah looked around at them all with wide eyes, ending with Celie.

Rolf and Pogue looked at Celie, too. So did Lulath. She was looking at the ancient griffin. The collar around its neck was of the same make as the rings and crown. The Arkower was like a shadow in the corners of her mind.

The wild griffins. The Castle, in distress, waiting back in Sleyne.

"We need to take the crown and ring with us," Celie said finally. "Also the griffin's collar."

"No, no, no!" Lilah took a step back, tugging Celie's sleeve so that she followed. "That is a very bad idea. We are not grave robbers!"

"I agree with Celie. And we'd be doing it for the good of the Castle and our family," Rolf said.

"We've gotten along for hundreds of years without these things," Lilah protested. "If they had any real power, don't you think the Arkower would have taken them by now, anyway?"

"You saw Ethan refuse to come in," Celie said. "This place is sacred to him." Her stomach made a little queasy motion at this, but she pushed it down. "It's very likely that none of them would dare to touch the king." Another queasy flop, but again she reminded herself of how much good they could do with the ring and the crown.

Or so she hoped.

"Our Lilah, we must be doing this for Sleyne," Lulath said. "Or so is my thinking."

The others all nodded.

"And I'd feel safer if we took some of the weapons, too," Pogue said.

Pogue had spent the past few months helping their brother Bran, the Royal Wizard, study and catalog a gallery full of strange weapons and armor that had appeared one Tuesday. Now they went to the rack of weapons in the tomb, and Pogue pointed out the ones that he recognized.

There were long rods that shot lightning bolts from the tip and gilded gauntlets that burned whoever the wearer touched. There were blades shaped like serpents and leaves, and bows that curved so fancifully that if she didn't know better, Celie would have thought they were purely decorative. After some discussion, though, they decided not to take the weapons. The swords would only provoke the Arkower and his people, if they saw strangers with them, and Pogue wasn't entirely certain he knew how to use the lightning weapons.

Not only that, but Lilah sat down on a gilt-covered stool and refused to go with them if they took a single dagger.

So in the end Celie took the ring from the king's finger, the crown from his head, and the collar from the griffin's neck. The others watched, hands folded and heads bowed in respect, as she did so. She carefully wrapped the precious relics in embroidered silk that Lilah found and put them in a leather purse that was among the more practical treasures of the tomb.

"I still say this is wrong," Lilah fretted as they left.

"Anything to help us get home," Rolf said.

"Anything to heal the Castle," Celie corrected him, wiping her hands on her skirts again. She hadn't liked touching the king, or his griffin, but it had been her idea, after all.

"But we don't know that," Lilah insisted. "The relics might do nothing at all, and all we've done is desecrate this poor man's tomb."

"Well, they're doing nothing here," Pogue said roughly. "And I feel like we've finally made steps toward getting home."

"Is that being one of the many fine weapons of which you and the wizard Bran are discovering the secrets thereof?" Lulath asked, pointing to one of the lightning spears.

"Yes," Pogue said, giving it a last longing look.

"It enthralls me!" Lulath said.

"That is hardly reassuring," Lilah muttered as they turned to go.

But Celie stopped. They were on the other side of the tapestry now, the one that made a wall between the biers and the treasure. In the Arkower's caves there were also walls made of tapestries.

But these tapestries were different. These tapestries looked just like the ones in the Castle. There were people, tall and pale, with golden hair like Celie's, and griffins frolicking at their feet. The Arkower's tapestries had been more angular and stylized, much like the cape that Lilah wore. There had been tapestries like that in the Castle, too, but only a few. Celie had found them in the newest parts of the Castle, the ones that had recently arrived in Sleyne and had never been seen before.

"What is it?" Pogue asked.

"It's nothing," Celie said. "I think."

Still carrying torches they walked silently out of the Tomb of the Builder, and closed and wrestled the latch back into place behind them.

It was dark now, the clearing filling with shadow. Rufus and his father were both snoring, none the worse for having been left behind.

Not that they had been alone. In the torchlight, Ethan's eyes were wide with fear. His gaze immediately found the leather bag Celie carried, and what little color there was in his face leaked right out of it.

"What did you take?" His voice was low, and he almost choked on the words. "What have you done?"

"You see?" Lilah said. "You see, we've done something horrible and sacrilegious." She took a few steps closer to Ethan. "I'm really sorry, I didn't want to, but they all voted to take some things and . . ."

"We need these things, we really do," Rolf put in. "Or we wouldn't have done this. We didn't intend to disturb anything, but—" He shrugged.

"I—I understand," Ethan said after a long pause. He took a deep breath. "You should probably come and see what I just found, too."

And he turned and led them away through the trees.

"Wonderful. Now I'm actually regretting that I didn't take that crossbow we saw," Lilah grumbled.

Chapter 10

I went into the trees to . . . ah . . . ," Ethan said. He turned bright red.

"Oh, I see," Rolf said.

Celie giggled nervously.

"Anyway . . . ?" Rolf prompted.

"Yes, well," Ethan went on. "That's when I saw it." He pointed, and they all took a few more steps forward.

Lying at the base of a large tree, in the hollow between its roots, was a nest of dried ferns and twigs. The nest would have been big enough for Celie to curl up inside, if it wasn't already occupied. Right in the middle of the nest was an egg. It was orange, a darker orange than Rufus's and Lorcan's eggs had been, but smaller than either of them.

"A griffin's egg," Lilah breathed. "I've never seen one." Then she flinched and looked around. "We'd better leave before the mother gets back. Mother birds can be vicious if you disturb their nests, and I can't imagine what a griffin might do!"

"There is no mother," Ethan said. He was standing off to one side, half-hidden by a clump of ferns. There was a funny look on his face.

"I think he's right," Pogue said. "Look at how dirty it is."

Celie looked, and felt her face screwing up with worry. Rufus hadn't had a mother, either, except for her, and Lorcan had been taken from his original nest to the Arkower's caves. So she really couldn't say what a well-tended egg in the wild should look like.

But this did not look like a well-tended egg. There was dirt and grit stuck to one side as though the wind had blown against it, and bits of leaves that had drifted down from the trees above. A few marks in the soil around the nest might have been griffin tracks, but they weren't fresh, even to Celie's untrained eye. The more she looked, the more she became convinced that the egg had been abandoned.

"The poor dear!" Lilah went forward to put one hand on the egg, and then drew it back. "Oh, it's hot!"

"So the egg is still alive?" Ethan asked. "I was afraid to check."

"Well, it's very warm," Lilah said. She looked at her little sister. "Celie?"

Celie went forward and put her hands on the egg, trying to choke back the lump in her throat as she remembered finding Rufus's egg all those months ago. This was not the same, she told herself firmly.

"It feels alive," Celie said.

And it did. It was uncomfortably warm to the touch, and Celie felt the tiniest of vibrations. She rocked it a little, and it rocked back. Lilah flinched.

"Don't make it hatch," she said, clutching Celie's arm.

"I'm not," Celie told her. "I'm just checking it. I used to roll Rufus around; I think he liked it." The lump rose in her throat again.

"I want to try," Rolf said eagerly. He came forward and put his own hands on the egg. "It's so warm! And I think I can feel something moving inside!" He gently rocked the egg as Celie had done.

"That's a pity," Ethan said.

"Why?" Celie looked at him sharply. He was the only one of them that hadn't come closer to the nest. He was standing, half-concealed by foliage, with that strange look on his face.

"What have you done?" Pogue demanded.

"I haven't done anything," Ethan said. "But someone else has."

He stepped out of the ferns and gestured for them to look behind where he'd been standing. A sudden premonition came over Celie, and she didn't think she wanted to see what he'd found. She looked at Rolf, who took her arm and moved a little in front of her.

"Do I really *want* to see this?" Lilah asked, echoing Celie's thoughts.

"I am thinking that this answer would be no," Lulath said softly, his gaze also on Ethan.

He, Rolf, and Pogue nodded to one another in that infuriating way boys have before they stepped over to the ferns, keeping Lilah and Celie behind them for protection. Celie bit back a smart remark: she was twelve years old, after all! But at the same time she really didn't want to see whatever they were looking at, especially after Pogue looked, went pale, and swore. Rolf uttered a wordless cry, and then something that sounded like a quick prayer.

"Oh, the beautiful mother," Lulath said. He shook his head and Celie saw tears in the corners of his eyes. "The beautiful mother!"

Seeing their reactions, Celie started to turn away, but then she couldn't help herself. She knew what was on the other side of the ferns but she had to see it with her own eyes. She slipped out of Rolf's grip and peered over the clump of ferns.

There, in a small clearing, was a dead griffin. Her golden fur and feathers appeared tarnished, her body limp and frail. There were three black arrows sticking out of her side and neck. And insects—

Celie ran back to the egg. She rested her hands on the poor unhatched orphan and breathed deeply, doing her best not to vomit. A minute later Lilah joined her.

"Well," Lilah said. She cleared her throat. Then, to Celie's shock she turned her head and spit noisily like one of the stable hands. "Well. That is . . . that is really, really horrible, and I hope whoever shot that griffin meets a terrible fate of their own."

"It was recent," Ethan said calmly. "In the last couple of days."

"That's nice," Lilah said bitterly. "Although I'm not sure how that helps, exactly."

"So now we must be worrying that this person of horror-bility is here in the forest near to us?" Lulath looked around nervously.

"Yes," Pogue said. "We need to get far away from here." He took Lilah's arm and tried to draw her away.

"But what about the egg?" Rolf joined Celie and Lilah at the nest and gave the egg another playful rock. It twitched under their hands. "Is it close to hatching, Cel?"

"It might be," she said. "I mean, it feels just like Rufus did . . . but I don't know if griffin eggs are like that the whole time they're eggs or just at the end. And I don't know how long they are in the eggs, either." She raised her eyebrows at Ethan.

"They're warm and they move the last two months, and it takes four months for them to hatch," he said. He sighed heavily and bent down to pick up a rock. "It's a royal griffin, so this is really a shame." He raised the rock.

Lilah screamed and Pogue lunged at Ethan, grabbing his hand and forcing him to drop the rock. Rolf threw himself to his knees and shielded the egg with his body.

"Are you mad?" Rolf shouted over his shoulder.

"You would be killing this only precious egg?" Lulath was angrier than Celie had ever heard him. The tall prince's face was red with rage, and he stepped toward Ethan with one hand on his belt knife, Lorcan hanging out of his tunic and hissing.

"We have to," Ethan protested, taking a step back but not releasing the rock. "Who's going to take care of it? Its mother is dead; we can't stay here until it hatches! It's just going to die!"

Celie reached around Rolf and patted the egg to reassure it. Then she stepped out of the nest, facing Ethan squarely. He didn't know where to look: at Pogue, who still held him; at Lulath, who had half drawn his belt knife; or at Celie, who was so beyond anger that she felt almost numb.

"Who shot the mother?" Celie asked him.

"I've been in the mountain for days," Ethan said, his eyes rolling. Pogue had let go of his wrist but was now pinning Ethan against a tree with his calloused hands, gripping the slighter youth's shoulders.

"That isn't what I asked," Celie said. Her voice was soft and she was pleased at how much it sounded like her father's, right before he unleashed the royal temper, as Rolf always termed it. "I asked you who shot her."

"I don't know," Ethan said.

Pogue's hands tightened on his shoulders, and Ethan squeaked.

"You're so clearly lying," Pogue snarled.

"I'm not! I don't know!" Ethan said, and then he whimpered a little as Pogue pressed harder.

Celie disliked lying, but she had had to do it on occasion in the past. To Prince Khelsh and the Council, when they tried to take over the Castle. To her parents and her tutor, when she'd been hiding a griffin in her rooms. Whenever possible, she tried to tell some of the truth, to make her lies seem more believable and to feel less awful about lying in the first place. She thought she saw that same look on Ethan's face that she had felt on her own when she told a "half lie."

"So, you don't know the exact person who did it," she said, squinting at him. "But you know about them. Or others like them. You know something. Tell us!"

"Who told you to break the egg?" Lilah wanted to know. She looked as though she was about to pick up a rock of her own to throw. "Why would you do something like that unless someone had ordered you to?"

Ethan looked away from them all and mumbled.

"What was that?" Rolf straightened up, adjusting his tunic. "I don't think I caught that," he said, his voice heavy with sarcasm.

"Tharkower," Ethan muttered.

"Speak up," Lilah snapped.

"He said the Arkower, didn't he, Pogue?" Celie said.

Pogue nodded, but Celie didn't need him to confirm it. She'd known that was what Ethan was going to say.

"The Arkower?" Lilah put her hands on her hips. "Why would he tell you to destroy any eggs you find?"

"I have never—not ever—broken an egg, I swear," Ethan hurried to say. "But he says that if you find eggs that cannot be brought back to the mountain, you should destroy them. If it hatches all alone, it will starve to death. And . . . well . . . you saw that we're trying to bond with them. But the mothers . . . don't like it."

"Someone killed the mother so they could take the egg to the Arkower, didn't they?" Lilah still sounded as though she might be sick.

"Yes," Ethan whispered.

"Then why didn't they take the egg?"

"I don't know," he said. His face was burning with shame, and he couldn't look in any of their eyes. "I guess something happened to them."

"Good," Celie said. "I hope the father griffin ate them."

"Celie!" But then Lilah shook her head, unable to pretend shock. "No, you're right, I hope something horrible happened to them." She put both hands to her head and started to pace around the nest. "What will we do? We simply can't leave the egg here to die!"

"You know," Rolf said, "you read stories when you're little, and you think it would be so amazing to have adventures happen to you. Then you actually go on one, and find out that it's awful. Nothing but bad food, sleeping cold on the hard ground, and treachery."

Pogue snorted.

"Well, if this is to be our very adventure, then we must be taking him hostages," Lulath said. He calmly began removing the decorative laces that ran down the side of his right trouser leg. "Hold him for only the moment more, friend Pogue! I will be tying his hands with this!"

"What? Why? I haven't done anything," Ethan protested.

"Except lie, and try to smash that poor egg," Celie retorted.

"I haven't! I only . . ." Ethan sagged. "Please," he whispered. "Please forgive me. Please take me with you."

All of Celie's anger left her. He looked so *broken*. And she couldn't imagine what his life had been like living all those years with the Arkower, always being told you would get a griffin, and then having griffins reject you.

"I can see what you're thinking," Rolf said softly.

"He helped you escape," Celie pointed out.

"This is being true," Lulath said.

"I don't trust him," Pogue argued.

"We don't need to trust him," Rolf said, ever practical. "We just need to keep him with us to make sure he doesn't go running to the Arkower. And I suppose he doesn't need to be tied up for that."

Celie squinted at Ethan. "You're a terrible liar," she told him. "So I want you to look me in the eye and promise me that you will not go running to the Arkower. That you want nothing more than to return to Sleyne with us."

Ethan looked Celie straight in the eyes and said, "I

swear that I will not betray you. I only want to go to Sleyne, and be where the Castle is."

There was silence for a moment, broken only by the rasping sound of Lorcan scraping his beak on one of the silver buttons on Lulath's tunic. Finally Rolf clapped his hands.

"Good enough for me, then," he said.

"As easy as can it be," Lulath said, slapping Pogue on the back as Pogue released Ethan with a faint growl. "Now, what are we to be doing with that poor sad egg?"

"Er," said Rolf. "Well. I know what I'd *like* to do."

"What's that?" Pogue had taken a few steps away from Ethan but was still watching him carefully.

"I want to take it with us," Rolf said.

This was greeted with more silence, a stunned silence.

"What if it breaks?" Lilah demanded. "What if the father comes after us? What if it *hatches*?"

Rolf poked at a hole in his tunic in thought. "If a griffin comes after us, and we think it's the father or aunt or uncle or grandmother, we can just give them the egg," he said reasonably. "It seems pretty thick shelled, and I bet we could make a sling for it from our tunics."

"And if it hatches?" Pogue's voice had an edge to it. "I know what you're thinking, Rolf!"

"What? What is he thinking?" Then Lilah answered her own question. *"You want to keep it?"*

"Why not?" Rolf said to Lilah. "Celie has a griffin, and

now Lulath has a griffin! And if Celie can raise a griffin practically by herself . . . no offense, Cel, but you are younger than I am . . . then why can't I?"

"None taken," Celie murmured. "You'd be a fine griffin rider," she told Rolf in a louder voice.

It was quickly decided. While Celie woke Rufus and his father, whom she had started calling Lord Griffin in her head, Rolf and Pogue took off their outer tunics, wrapped the egg up, and tied it to Rolf's back with Lilah's sash. Celie and Ethan kept watch on the lake, nervously waiting for any sign of the Arkower.

"We can be doing this," Lulath said with enthusiasm. "An egg to hatch! A new griffin! Such the adventure for us, we must be writing it down when we are returned to the Castle!"

Celie smiled. She felt the pouch at her waist and wondered what it would be like when they returned to the Castle triumphantly bearing an egg, a baby griffin, and a crown and ring for her father.

If only they could find the missing piece of the Eye. Celie was sure it wasn't in the Castle back in Sleyne, but she had a definite hunch that it was in the ruins somewhere. That was where the griffins lived, after all. And that was why, she suspected, the Castle had become more capricious and started moving more rooms to Sleyne. It had started waking up long before she and Rolf began collecting evidence of griffins being real and putting it in the holiday feasting hall.

The Arkower's nephew, Wizard Arkwright, had scolded Rolf and Celie for "distressing" the Castle by reminding it of its past. He had protested their putting tapestries, maps, and books with depictions of griffins in the feasting hall, which was actually the Heart of the Castle, and tried to hide the Eye from them as well. But now the Eye was in its place, and Celie was sure that if its missing piece was anywhere in Sleyne, the Castle would have found a way to tell her father by now.

"Ethan," Celie said as Pogue made some final adjustments to Rolf's burden. "You stole the piece of the Eye, right?"

"Yes," he said, looking uncomfortable. "I thought I was doing the right thing!"

She waved aside his protest. "It's not that . . . You know what it looks like!"

"Well, yes," he admitted.

"Good, you can help me find it."

Chapter
11

⤙ ⟿

They kept to the thin trees at the start of the forest and made remarkably good time back to the Castle ruins, considering their exhaustion and the unwieldy bundle that Rolf was carrying. At the base of the hatching tower, Rufus's father left them, and they all took a moment to catch their breath and look around.

"I can't believe the Arkower didn't beat us here," Rolf said. He stretched to ease his back. "Do you think that Rufus could take this up there for me?" he asked Celie. "I don't think I can face all those stairs."

"I'm sure," Celie said. "He's anxious to fly."

Rufus had followed his father a little ways across the broken courtyard, but at the sound of his name he came romping back. Celie chirruped at him and he butted his head into her middle. She led him over to Rolf, but the egg was fastened so tightly that he couldn't get it off his back.

"Just fly up with Rufus and the egg," Lilah said in frustration, after breaking a nail trying to pick apart one of the knots. Pogue glanced over, but he and Lulath were busy asking Ethan about where they could find food.

"Oh, right," Rolf said.

"Here, boy," Celie said. "Take Rolf up to the tower."

"What is that you have, Crown Prince Rolf?" the Arkower called out as he sauntered out of the trees. "An egg? We must bring it back to my cavern, where it can hatch in peace and safety." He smiled at them, looking like a kindly grandfather.

Rufus hissed. He slammed his body into Celie and she fell across his back. Lilah screamed, and Lulath shouted something in Grathian that Celie didn't catch. She was too busy hanging on as Rufus took off into the air. She grabbed his harness, nearly slipping backward and landing on her head as Rufus shot toward the open windows of the tower. She shouted for him to take her back, but he ignored her and dropped her on the floor.

Celie leaped to her feet and ran for the window, but Rufus blocked her way. She wrestled with him, trying to shove him aside so that she could see what was happening below, but he wouldn't budge. She yanked on the harness and shouted at him, but he just kept squawking and batting his wings at her. The pouch at her waist came loose, and the ring dropped out.

"What are you doing?" Celie yelled. She clapped her

113

hands, trying to shoo him away, and he lashed out with one talon, scratching her palm. "Ouch!"

Rufus cowered at her feet, frightened. Celie flapped her hand and then sucked at the cut. She stomped her foot against the pain, and Rufus backed into a corner, crying. She felt the crown at her hip slipping out of the pouch and grabbed it. One of the prongs dug into her cut and she shrieked again, reflexively tossing the crown across the room.

The clang it made when it hit the wall rang in Celie's head. She felt the strange sensation that meant the Castle had changed something. But that was impossible! This tower was—

"It's alive!"

Celie slapped her hands against the floor, listening with her whole body, and there was no mistaking the warmth and faint hum of the living Castle. She jumped up and ran to one of the windows, and this time Rufus didn't stop her. Her elation was short-lived as she looked down to the courtyard and saw . . . nothing.

The others were all gone.

"Lilah," Celie screamed. "Rolf! Pogue! Lulath!"

No one answered.

From the distance, she heard another griffin cry, and she saw a form she thought was Rufus's mother circling over the trees, but she couldn't be sure. She shouted until she was hoarse, but they were all gone, even Ethan and the Arkower.

Slumping back onto the tower floor, Celie looked at her griffin. Suitably contrite, he crept over and laid his head in her lap. She stroked his feathers absently.

"We have a living tower," she said to him. "But I'm afraid to ask the Castle to take us home. What if it never brings back the others?"

Rufus carked.

"Exactly," she said. "I suppose they ran off when the Arkower came. I'll just bet your father helped Rolf get the egg out of sight, and they're hiding in the forest now." She was trying to give herself courage, and she almost succeeded.

"I'm not going to just sit here until they come back," she decided aloud after a moment. "There are things to do: find the Eye, get back to Sleyne. We have one live tower, why not two?" She gently pushed Rufus off her lap and stood up.

He cocked his head at her and preened for a moment before standing. He shook out his wings while Celie gathered up the crown, checking it carefully to make certain that it hadn't sustained any damage when she threw it. It appeared to be unharmed, so she tucked it back into the pouch, snatched up the ring and dropped it into the pouch as well, and climbed on Rufus's back.

"To the tower," she told him, pointing alongside his head so he could see where she meant. "The other tower. Quick, now!"

Rufus didn't even have to flap his wings. He just glided over the courtyard to the tower and perched on the windowsill. Celie didn't bother to dismount; she pulled the crown out of her bag and tapped it against the window frame. It made a tinking sound, but nothing else. There was no echoing clang, no shudder that ran through the mortar of the tower. She did it again, a little more firmly this time, and winced at the sound that told her she had dented the crown. But it still wasn't the sound she had been waiting for, and the tower still didn't respond.

Rufus climbed through the window and Celie hopped off his back. She slipped the ring on her right thumb before she crouched on the floor and tapped the crown against the flagstones, but there was still nothing. She looked around nervously in the dim tower, tucked the crown under one arm, and wiped her grimy palms on her equally grimy skirt. Then she took the crown and tossed it across the room.

It made a satisfying clatter hitting the floor. But the tower didn't wake up.

"What are we going to do?" Celie said aloud.

Unlike the crown, her voice echoed in the empty tower, which made her angry. She stomped across the floor, found the crown, shook the ring off her thumb, and threw them both across the room for good measure. The ring pinged off the wall and fell to the floor. The crown hit the floor with a hollow thud and rolled against the wall.

Rufus cocked his head to the side at the thud the crown made. Celie did, too, then remembered the trapdoor in the floor. The hatching towers that were attached to the Castle now had wide low doors in the wall, but the doors

116

in the two dead towers were bricked over and a rough trap-door in the floor of each led to a spiral staircase. Celie walked over and stomped on the trapdoor a few times, her brain whirling.

Someone had altered these towers since the Castle had left them behind. Someone had been living in them, or using them, but the Arkower had said that they didn't live in the ruins; they only provided things for the feasts. Was that why this tower wouldn't wake up? Who had made the trapdoor? She stomped on the door again as she thought.

From below, someone knocked back.

Chapter
12

⟞⟐⟝

Celie screamed and leaped backward. Rufus lunged, clawing at the door and shrieking his battle cry. From beneath the floor came the sound of shouts and pounding, and then someone tried to open the trapdoor. It didn't work very well because Rufus was standing on top of the door, but they kept trying and shouting in a language that Celie didn't know.

Finally her curiosity got the better of her fear, and she grabbed Rufus by the harness and hauled him back. Rufus protested loudly but he moved, and then the door flew open. Celie was temporarily blinded by the lantern that the person carried, and so was Rufus, judging by the way he cried out and buried his head in her skirts.

When her vision cleared she found herself looking down at a wizened little man. He was standing a few steps down from the tower room and holding a globular brass lantern.

His eyes were so faded that Celie couldn't tell what color they were, and the robe he wore was much the same. His beard was so long that it actually disappeared down into the stairway, by which Celie judged it to fall at least to his knees.

"Hello?" Celie said. "Do you live here?"

"A girl!" He gaped at her. "What is a girl doing in this old tower?" His eyes flicked to Rufus, but he seemed to be talking mostly to himself.

"You speak Sleynth, too?" Celie asked, even though it was a rather silly question. She could hear him speaking Sleynth, though he had a heavy accent.

"She speaks to me, and in the language I am speaking," the old man said, appearing to address the wall. "Shall I answer? Perhaps. And in that way I could ask more questions of her."

"Yes," Celie said. "I'll tell you whatever I can if you'll answer my questions, too." She took a tiny step toward the old man. He was a little senile, certainly, but he didn't seem to mean any harm.

"She's talking to me first. I suppose it's impolite now to ask her name," the old man said.

"My name is Princess Cecelia of Sleyne," Celie said in the bright voice she used with Lulath's dogs. "What's yours?"

"Sleyne? That place where the Castle has taken itself?" Now the old man was truly talking to her. Though the color of his eyes had faded to a nondescript shade, when they focused on her, Celie found that his gaze was very sharp indeed.

"Yes, that's right," Celie said. "I grew up in Castle Glower. My father is the king of Sleyne."

The old man made a gesture as though brushing aside her words. "There is no Castle Glower. There is only the Castle."

"Yes," Celie said, nodding broadly. "It is the best castle," she offered, not sure what to say.

"It is *the* Castle," he told her sharply. "Nothing else matters." He studied her. "And your father guards it?"

"Er. Yes . . . ?"

The man made a rude noise, as though he doubted King Glower's ability to keep the Castle safe. He pointed to the crown that Celie was still holding.

"He can't do much without that," he said.

Offended, Celie drew herself up to her full height. With the old man on the stairs, she was taller than him, which she felt gave her the advantage. She put her hands on her hips, which was rather spoiled by the awkward way the crown was now sticking out over her wrist.

"My father is King Glower the Seventy-ninth, and he is a very good king! The Castle loves him—it loves our entire family! My father is the tenth of our family to be king."

The old man shook his head as though her words were flies buzzing around his ears. "You must take him the crown," the old man said a moment later. "And the ring."

He pointed to Celie's tightly clenched left fist, and she

blushed. She'd been trying to hide the ring, but she was clearly holding *something*, since she'd had to loop the handle of Rufus's harness over her forearm to keep him back. Her knuckles were slowly turning white from holding the ring. "It was a mistake for them to be kept back." He shook his head again. As if speaking to himself, he said, "She could have taken the Eye if it had not been lost. They must suffer, he must pay."

So the crown and the ring really could help . . . or so it seemed. Had the Arkower kept them back along with the Eye? Why?

Celie blinked a few times, not sure what to do or say. "Who are you?" she finally remembered to ask.

"I? I am an old man. I used to be a wizard. I used to be a lot of things . . ." He turned his attention to Rufus. "That is a fine griffin. Not full grown, of course."

"He's four months old," Celie said.

"Very large for his age, then," the old man said. He pursed his lips. "He's of the king's line." He nodded. "I thought that they had an egg. They hid it so well." His head bobbed up and down. "And why not? I am too old to take care of it. Though you are perhaps too young."

"Did you say the king's line? What king?" Celie's heart was fluttering, and she thought she knew that answer already.

"The king of the griffins, who roosts even now in the stables that once housed his army," the old man said, rocking back and forth and speaking in a singsong. The lantern

121

light flickered across the walls. "With his beautiful, beautiful queen. Who has not gifted the world with an egg in long, so long, because who is there to raise it up and train it to battle? Only I, I and my ancient enemy, that monster in the mountain, and him they will not give an egg to."

"The monster in the . . . do you mean the Arkower?" Celie wanted to shake her head, her thoughts were buzzing around so crazily that it felt as though there were flies in *her* ears now.

"The Arkower!" The old man wheezed with laughter. "The *Arkower*! Oh, the drama of it all! It is better than a pantomime for the winter feast!" The lantern shook so much that Celie hurried to stow the crown so that she might take the lantern from him. But he lifted it out of her reach, still chortling. "I'm not so far gone I cannot hold my own lantern," he told her. "The Arkower! His name is Nathanal," the old man said. "A plain name, but an honest one. Fitting that he got rid of it, the dishonest *balagaha*." He shook his head, and then rocked a little as though the motion had made him dizzy.

"Balagaha?"

"Don't use such foul language," the old man clucked. "It's unbecoming to a young lady, and a princess besides!"

Celie mentally stored the word away for later use.

"The Arkower's name is Nathanal?" She brought her mind back to the more important information.

"Indeed," the old man said. "It means 'of the soil' in Arkish, but if he has ever worked an honest day in his life,

I will eat that griffin." He hooted with laughter, startling Rufus.

Celie tugged Rufus back to her side, putting the ring in the pouch beside the crown so that she could keep a better grip on him. "And what is *your* name?"

The old man looked almost as startled as Rufus had. "My name? I . . . No one has asked my name in centuries," he said, and Celie saw that his mind had retreated again.

"I'm sorry," Celie said politely. "If you'd rather not tell me, that's all right."

"Pffft," he said, flapping a hand. "I'm not keeping my name from you to make more of myself than I am, like some wizards! I just haven't . . . haven't spoken to anyone in *yeonks* of time."

Celie stored that away as well. Yeonks of time. She liked the sound of it.

"Bratsch," the old man blurted out.

"I beg your pardon?" Celie caught her mind wandering almost as badly as the old man's. "I mean, bless you!"

"That's my name," he said, looking annoyed. "Bratsch."

Celie turned red to the roots of her hair. "I'm sorry, it's . . . a very nice name."

"It means 'musician' in Hathelocke," Bratsch said with a shrug. "A foolish name for one marked as a wizard from birth."

Celie slumped against Rufus, trying to catch these buzzing thought-flies. "You . . . you're a wizard . . . and a Hathelocke?"

"What did you think I was, a green horse? In these robes?" He snorted and gestured at his dust-colored, patched garments.

"I—I—" Celie stammered. The old man's rags bore about as much resemblance to her brother Bran's robes as Rufus the griffin did to Rufus the stuffed lion.

"It doesn't matter," Bratsch said, waving a hand at her. "What matters is what a little girl from Sleyne is doing here in the ruins of the Castle . . . ?"

"That *is* what matters!" Celie leaped on this moment of sanity. "Yes! You are correct, sir! I need to get back to Sleyne, but with my friends and siblings who are here with me. There are six of us, and we all must get back to Sleyne as soon as we can!"

"Of course you must, you don't want to get the plague!"

"No," Celie agreed. "We certainly don't! Is it true that it comes from the lake?"

"Oh, yes!" Bratsch said, and spat to the side as though he'd tasted something foul. "Nathanal's pride and joy: the curse of the lake! One dip of your tiniest toe, and you'll be dead within a week." He wiped his mouth with a dingy sleeve.

"He *created* it?" Celie rocked back against Rufus. The Arkower had created the plague on purpose? "But why . . . why? And how is it possible to keep it cursed all these years?" Celie asked.

"Renews it every year, doesn't he? Vicious *bolugur*," Bratsch snarled.

"He . . . what?" A curse . . . and he renewed it every year? But who was left for it to kill, except his own people?

"Why?" Her voice quavered. "Why would he do such a thing?"

Bratsch shook his head, his lined face even more creased with sorrow. "If Nathanal and his people can't have control of the Castle, then it is better if they all die." He spat again. "Or so he says."

Celie was now all but sitting on Rufus, her legs trembling so badly that they could hardly hold her up. She didn't even know what to say, what question to ask next. It was all too much. After all, it had been less than three days since she'd even found out about the plague and the Glorious Arkower, and now this strange old wizard was telling her that most of what she'd thought she'd learned was wrong.

"But they do control the Castle . . . they sent it to Sleyne," Celie said. "Didn't they? You need to . . . tell me everything," she finally gasped out.

"I think I need to get you a drink of something strong and a warm blanket," Bratsch said, giving her a pragmatic look that reminded her very much of Bran.

"I'm not allowed to have wine or spirits," Celie replied, wishing she didn't sound quite so prim, but knowing that her mother would confine her to her room for years if she did drink.

"A warm blanket and a drink of something without wine or spirits, then," the wizard agreed. "Come this way." He started down the rickety stairs. "Will she follow me?

125

Do I want her to?" Wizard Bratsch started muttering to himself as he went.

"I—I can't," Celie called after him, barely stopping herself from saying that she *wouldn't*. She supposed that it wasn't his fault he'd become senile, but still . . . "Rufus doesn't fit," she explained, and stiffened her resolve.

"Fly him down to the base of the tower," Bratsch called back, irritated, and kept on stumping down the stairs.

Celie and Rufus looked at each other. She fingered the pouch at her waist for a moment, wondering if she should try to wake the tower again, but decided against it. For now. Bratsch had answers that she needed, and they had at least one live tower to work with. She mounted Rufus, and he flew out the window without any urging.

Below them Wizard Bratsch hobbled across the broken stones of the courtyard. Celie guided Rufus down to walk alongside the old man.

Bratsch left the ruins and went into the encroaching forest. Only a little way in was a small wooden house. It was one room; the three of them barely fit inside. The only furnishings were a bed and a rough fireplace made of rounded stones. Celie thought this very strange. There were cut stones from the Castle all around, so why hadn't he built a stone house, or at least used them for a chimney? But when she asked the wizard, he just shook his head.

"I cannot take the bones of the Castle," he said.

"I guess that's a good idea," Celie agreed. "I woke up the

other tower just now, and I was trying to wake up the one where you found me."

"Brave girl," the wizard said. "Good girl. It will pain me to see the last of the Castle go far away, but I think it is time." He sighed. "Bones and stones, gone and gone and gone."

"Can you help me wake the other tower? And the other parts, too?" Celie's heart pounded. "And then send it all to Sleyne?"

The old man sucked at his teeth and rocked back and forth, sitting on the rough hearth. "Gone the bones, gone the stones," he muttered. "Sleyne Sleyne Sleyne. Why not?"

"You can?"

"Yes, that will be simple." He looked at her with eyes that appeared quite lucid. "As simple as finding your own foot."

Celie smiled at him and ignored this last comment. "So you'll help me get my brother and sister and our friends away from the Ark—from Wizard Nathanal?"

"Here is some hot tea," the old man said evasively, ladling something out of a pot on the fire. He handed the wooden cup to Celie, and a smell of rose hips wafted from it.

"How did you learn Sleynth?" Celie asked, blowing on the tea to make sure it was cool enough to drink.

"I did not just send the Castle any which place," Bratsch said indignantly. "I went to many worlds before I chose yours. Sleyne was no more than a dot on the map, some farms in a forest, with their foolish unicorns frolicking in a meadow." He winked conspiratorially. "Our people would find it easy to prosper."

"But didn't you worry that the griffins would try to eat the unicorns?" Celie shifted uncomfortably and took a sip of tea; though she was a little pleased at the way he'd said "our people." "Because they did. If you were wondering."

"Did they?" Bratsch didn't look all that interested. Instead he busied himself getting a bowl of water for Rufus and a blanket for Celie. "Hmph. But the unicorns could not eat the griffins, that was the concern. The griffins were the concern. All the concern. The root of the problem. The root." He pursed his lips. "The root. The heart. The eye."

"What did you say?" Celie asked.

"I said the griffins could not be eaten by unicorns," the old man retorted.

"But they all died," Celie felt compelled to say. "The griffins and their riders still died from the plague or curse or whatever it was."

"Did they?" Bratsch's face went rigid for a moment, and he stared off into the distance. "Well. But the Castle survives. And this one survives." He pointed at Rufus.

"Yes," Celie said. "And . . . and we found two more eggs. One's already hatched. We're going to take them back to Sleyne."

"No." Bratsch shook his head. "No, they should stay here. They die here, they die there, does it matter?"

Celie stared at him, feeling out-of-sorts. Didn't he want the griffins to have a chance? Rufus was healthy and happy—that was obvious to anyone who looked at him. Didn't Bratsch want the same for the other griffins?

"Their time has passed," Bratsch said. "They are better off here in the forest, if what you say is true."

Celie immediately wished she hadn't said anything about the unicorns or the plague. "But the Castle needs them," Celie protested.

"Nonsense," Bratsch said, clucking his tongue. "The Castle doesn't need anything! I designed it that way myself! It's best to have a strong man of our people to keep it under control, of course, but even that is unnecessary." Bratsch gazed off into the distance, a smile playing about his creased lips. "It needs nothing."

This annoyed Celie to no end. She loved the Castle. A year ago she would have said that she loved the Castle as much as her family. But now she had Rufus and Rufus's family. Lulath had Lorcan, and they had the orphaned egg. She couldn't leave them, and she doubted very much that the Castle would want her to. And if Bratsch had designed the Castle, then whose tomb had she robbed? She shook that thought off for a moment, however.

"The Castle is so amazing," Celie said hastily. She tried for flattery, to get some answers. "I never thought I would get to meet the man who built it! And now I'm here talking to you, but—"

"I didn't *build* it!" Bratsch snapped. "How old do you think I am?"

Celie felt her cheeks burn. "Um, old?" She wished Lilah were there. Lilah was much better at getting what she wanted from people.

Bratsch snorted. "My *grandfather* built the Castle! I merely altered it so that it would recognize our people once the Arkower attempted to take control."

Celie ran frantic fingers through her dirty hair, desperate to understand. "But the . . . Who are you . . . if the Arkower . . . Who is the Builder?"

If Bratsch was saying that he was a Hathelocke, and his grandfather had built the Castle . . . then was everything the Arkower and his nephew Arkwright told them a lie?

"I don't understand you," the old man scolded her. "Ask one question at a time!"

Celie tried to clear her thoughts. "Who built the Castle?"

"I told you: my grandfather did," Wizard Bratsch said, clearly annoyed at her inability to understand. "He was its first king, the one whose tomb contained the very crown you're holding, but everyone just called him the Builder."

"But he wasn't from the Glorious Arkower? I mean, here?"

"This is not the Glorious Arkower, no matter what that fool has told you," Bratsch said in a low, rage-filled voice that sent a rill of terror down Celie's spine. He glared at her from beneath his wild white brows. "This is *Hatheland*."

Chapter
13

It was too much for Celie. She put her head down on her knees for a moment and breathed deeply. Rufus nuzzled her hair, concerned, and she threw one arm around his neck. She felt as though she was trying to walk through oatmeal, or that her brain simply wasn't working properly.

"What is wrong with you? Are you ill?" Wizard Bratsch fussed around her, not quite touching her and offering no real comfort, just more of the bitter, too-hot tea. "She's ill. It's not the plague, I see no blisters, but what if she dies in my house? Bad luck! Bad luck! And then the griffin? What will it do if she is dead?"

"We didn't know," Celie wailed. "Do you understand me? *We didn't know there were real griffins!* Then I hatched Rufus, and I hid him, I was so scared . . . and Arkwright came . . . he told us the Castle came from the Glorious Ark-ower, that his people had been griffin riders but the griffins were dead . . . that the Castle was asleep and needed to stay asleep . . . then we came here and there's more griffins, and you say this is Hatheland, not the Glorious Arkower, and nothing we thought we knew is true, and I just don't know what to do."

Somewhere in the middle of her outburst, Bratsch had frozen, her half-full mug of tea in one hand. He was staring over her head, and his face was the color of clay. Then it very slowly began to fill with color until it was dark purple.

"Arkwright lives," he whispered. "Is that what she said?"

"Y-y-yes," Celie said, pulling Rufus closer.

"The young fool who nearly destroyed the Castle," Bratsch snarled. "The young fool who broke the Eye. The young fool who led the rebellion. He lives."

"Yes?" Celie was starting to feel sorry for Wizard Arkwright. The terrible expression on Wizard Bratsch's face was scaring *her*, and she wasn't a liar and a villain, as he was.

"And does he control the Castle?" Bratsch's eyes locked on Celie, and he looked perfectly lucid once more.

"No," Celie said, feeling relieved that she could offer that much consolation. "I told you: my father does."

"But does Arkwright control your father?"

Celie bristled. "No one controls my father," she snapped. "He is the king! None of us even knew Arkwright until a month ago. He's been avoiding the Castle for years."

"Ha! His guilt consumes him," Bratsch said with relish. "And he doesn't have a griffin?"

Celie shook her head.

"Then he has nothing!" Bratsch howled with vicious laughter. "No Castle, no griffin! Nothing!"

Celie opened her mouth to ask him to explain, not that she thought it would make the situation any clearer, but someone beat her to it.

"I think I missed most of that," Rolf said from the doorway. "Could you start from the beginning?"

"Rolf!" Celie flung herself at him.

Wizard Bratsch also flung himself at Rolf. "Who are you? Get out of my house!"

Pogue stepped forward and caught the old man's shoulder, keeping him at arm's length.

"I'm Crown Prince Rolf of Sleyne," Rolf shouted. Wizard Bratsch was berating Pogue in several languages. "I've been looking for my sister!" He pointed to Celie.

"Oh! You found me!" Celie hugged Rolf again. Then she hugged Pogue, who was finally able to release Wizard Bratsch, and gave her a crushing hug in return. "Where are Lulath and Lilah, though? Lorcan? And the egg?"

"We came back to get you," Rolf said. "Lilah and Lulath stayed in the forest. The big griffin is hiding them. Or something. He won't let them leave the clearing where he took us, anyway."

"He . . . took you?" Celie asked.

"When the Arkower appeared, he grabbed me in his talons—the griffin, not the Arkower—and lifted me off into the trees," Rolf said. "It was terrifying. He dropped me, but not very far from the ground, then flew off, and the next thing I know, he and his mate are back with the others, hiding us in a thicket in the forest until the Arkower left, I suppose."

"We tried to get him to take us back to the tower once it was safe," Pogue said. "But he brought us here instead." He looked around. "Clever animal."

"They are not animals, they are griffins," Bratsch said stiffly. "The girl said that one of you bonded with a griffin. Which of you was it?"

"Neither. It was our friend Prince Lulath of Grath," Rolf said. "He's hiding in the forest with our other sister, his griffin, and an egg. We need to get to them."

"Of Grath? Where is 'of Grath'? Another griffin has bonded with another stranger?" Wizard Bratsch looked disgusted. "Complication after complication! After so many years of quiet!"

"All right," Rolf said slowly. "You can see why we need to get back to them. But first of all, I really must know: Who are you, and what in the world were you just telling my sister?"

"There's another one of you wandering the forest with an egg?"

Wizard Bratsch didn't look at Rolf, but at Celie for confirmation. Celie nodded. The wizard turned to Rufus's father, whom he had earlier called the king of the griffins, and let out a shrill cry that raised the hair on Celie's arms.

Lord Griffin raised his wings and took several dancing steps forward. The elderly wizard spoke to him in some other language, something with lots of *th* sounds, and Celie wondered dazedly if it was the language of the Hathelockes. Lord Griffin set off into the night, and the wizard beckoned them back into his hut.

"Is he . . . sane?" Pogue muttered to Celie as they filed through the low door.

"I don't know," was all she could say.

She believed that Wizard Bratsch was telling the truth. But she didn't understand half of what he was saying. And not only that, she didn't like him. For a brief moment she'd thought he'd be better than the Arkower, and she'd started to think of him as the "good wizard," because anyone who wasn't the Arkower had to be good, or so she assumed. But in his own way he was just as selfish and possibly as evil as the Arkower, or Nathanal, or whatever his name was.

Bratsch made them as comfortable as he could. Celie ended up sitting on Rufus's back in order to make room, and Rufus was resting his head in Pogue's lap. The wizard gave them each a crude mug of extremely hot tea, and then settled himself on a stool that was practically *in* the fire, though that didn't seem to bother him in the slightest.

"If you don't mind, sir," Rolf said in his most polite voice. "We would very much like to know anything you can tell us about the Castle, the Glorious Arkower, Hatheland, and anything else you judge important."

"There is so much," Wizard Bratsch said, shaking his head. "Hundreds of years have passed since most of my Castle left this land."

"All the more reason to start at the beginning and tell us everything," Rolf said.

Wizard Bratsch gave him a cold look, and Rolf smiled back winningly.

"My grandfather was the Builder of the Castle," Wizard Bratsch said, diving in despite his annoyed expression. "It was to be a refuge for our people and their griffins, and so it was for many years. Our people and the griffins had been tied together since the dawn of the world, which made many jealous. We needed a stronghold to protect ourselves from our enemies, enemies like the Arkish.

"They were cave dwellers, savages," Wizard Bratsch snarled, and then spit into the fire. "They tried again and again to take the Castle, to take our griffins, and they failed and were beaten back into the mountains time after time. They tried to train the wild griffins, but they will not bond with a man the way our griffins will."

"What changed?" Pogue was leaning forward, one hand stroking Rufus's head, but his attention was completely on the wizard.

"They could not take the griffins, so they took the eggs," Wizard Bratsch said, his voice bleak. "One night during my grandfather's reign, their wizards worked a powerful spell and spirited away every griffin egg for miles around. A year later they attacked. Our beasts would not fight their brothers, their sisters, their own children!

"They can recognize them, yes, of course they can!"

Bratsch wagged his finger at Rolf before he even had a chance to ask.

"Rufus's parents know him," Celie reminded her brother.

Wizard Bratsch hissed at her to be silent. "The Arkish took the Castle and cast us out. They could not take away our griffins, but they kept the eggs, and we became exiles in our own land, living in the mountain like common trolls, while they pranced about our halls and called our land the Glorious Arkower!

"We took what we could: the crown, the rings . . ." The wizard gazed into the distance, looking back at his past. "My father was a great man and he took back what was ours! After a seemingly endless war we were returned to our Castle home, and given back our due place as the rulers of this land!"

His eyes glowed in the firelight. They reminded Celie of Rufus's eyes.

"That's . . . wonderful," Celie said.

"I made changes to the Castle, changes that would keep it ours forever," Bratsch continued. "I had only begun to cleanse the taint of the Arkish from our corridors when we were betrayed. My father had taken an Arkish wife in an attempt to make peace with them. It was his only mistake. My half brother, that Arkwright who you say still lives in Sleyne, worked with his mother's brother to create the plague. He is responsible for the deaths of thousands of our people, hundreds of griffins, also. Then he cracked the

Eye and tried to destroy the Castle. We had no choice but to send it away to try to protect it and the rest of our griffins."

"That's not what he—" Celie began, but Rolf put a hand on her elbow and gave it a little squeeze. "And we're descended from both, so—" Another squeeze, and she stopped.

"That's a horrible story," Rolf said. "What luck that any griffins survived!"

"Can I ask you something?" Pogue sounded almost timid. Wizard Bratsch gave a regal nod. "Why don't you have a griffin?"

The elderly man fumbled with the kettle for a moment. "I—I am a wizard," he told them. "I have my mind on other matters, and no time to train a beast."

"Ah," Pogue said.

Celie thought he sounded less than convinced. Which matched exactly how she felt. Either Bratsch was lying, or the Arkower was. Bratsch's story would explain the different types of tapestries and the Arkower's constant striving for new griffins for his people. But why were they still taking care of the Castle, if they were Arkish? Celie's head was spinning.

Rolf clearly felt the same. He stood up and clapped his hands, startling them all.

"Thank you so much for sharing this with us, Wizard Bratsch," Rolf said. "It is a great deal to take in. I think it best that we retire to one of the towers for the evening. If our sister is found by the griffin who rescued us, then that is where she will look for us."

"Oh, go, go!" Wizard Bratsch flapped his hands at them. "They come, they go, they do nothing. And what's to be done without it? Nothing," the old man muttered as they left.

✦ ✦ ✦

They picked their way silently through the ruins of the Castle, to the tower that Celie had awakened. She realized that she hadn't told them what she'd done, but decided to wait and see if they noticed. Rufus flew them up one at a time, Celie first, and she lit the lantern that Bratsch had given her.

Rolf looked around, surprised. "It's alive! Or awake, whichever it is." He ran a hand lovingly down one of the walls. "I wonder when that happened!"

"What?" Pogue knocked on the window frame. "Are you sure?"

"Positive."

"I did it," Celie told them excitedly. "It was me! I used the crown and woke this tower!"

"What?" Rolf gaped.

"It's true," Celie said. "I dropped the crown and it made the tower wake up!"

"That's amazing," Rolf said. "We should go do the other tower." He turned as though to go straight to it.

"I tried," Celie told him, deflating. "But it didn't work.

And then Wizard Bratsch found me . . . and well, you know the rest."

"Odd," Rolf commented. "We'll have to try again later. For now—"

"For now we have to try to sort through all those lies and half-truths," Pogue said grimly.

"Exactly," Rolf said with a sigh. "And hope that that other griffin brings Lulath and Lilah soon. And Ethan. Another mouth to feed . . ." He threw down some of the blankets they'd brought along and slumped down on them. "Well." He brightened. "I wonder if we could ask the Castle for some food now."

"We'll see about that," Pogue said. "But what about all we've learned?"

"The Hathelockes built the Castle," Celie said with surety.

"That explains the changes in the tapestries," Pogue agreed. "The old ones, by the hatching towers, must be Hathelocker . . . Hathelockish? And the fancier ones are Arkish?"

"The other way around, I think," Rolf said. "The ones that show people and griffins dancing around and hunting are Hathelocke. The ones that show people trying to bond with griffins are wishful thinking on the part of the Arkish. Most of the tapestries in the Castle are Hathelocke . . . if we're right. The ones that came with the hatching towers are Arkish."

"And then more happened," Celie said. She yanked some of the blankets out from under Rolf for herself.

"Then the Arkish fought the Hathelockes, took the Castle, and lived there," Rolf said. "That much is clear as well."

"But after that it's all . . ." Pogue shook his head, trailing off.

"I'm guessing no one had full control of the Castle after that," Rolf said. "It sounds like it was just endless betrayal and fighting."

"So the Arkish poisoned the lakes, but it was the Hathelockes who decided to leave for Sleyne," Celie said.

"But the Arkish broke the Eye," Pogue said.

"Which side should we be on?" Rolf asked.

"Neither," Pogue said with disgust.

"The Castle's," Celie retorted.

They all sat in silence for a long time. After a while Pogue climbed down and gathered wood for a fire. Celie reclined against Rufus, who had gone right to sleep, and was just starting to tip downward into an exhausted doze herself when Rolf spoke again. She jolted awake, and it took her a moment to realize what he was saying.

"Do you think the Castle made our parents get married to stop this war?"

"What?" Celie pried her eyes open. Pogue, who was sitting against the wall a little way away looked at her blankly. Rolf was staring at the far wall, the flickering lantern light making his face look ten years older.

"Mother's family are Hathelockes, and Father is Arkish, supposedly. Do you think the Castle made our parents get married to stop the war here?"

Celie thought about that. It took her a minute, but she thought she saw what Rolf was worrying about. Their parents had gotten betrothed after the Castle had locked them both in a room together for a day. "Maybe," she said finally. "But Daddy was the Crown Prince and Mummy was the daughter of the Royal Wizard, so it was a good match for Sleyne, too. And so many years after the war started, it seems strange."

"I know . . . but . . . I guess . . ." Rolf stumbled over the words.

"Are you worried the Castle will make *you* marry someone you don't like?" Celie asked, still a little puzzled. "Mummy says that she'd been in love with Daddy for years before the Castle put them together."

"I know," Rolf said, waving a hand to brush that away. "It's not that . . . All right, it's sort of that." He sighed. "I'll try not to worry too much about that unless I get locked in a room with some girl I don't know." He cleared his throat. "But I am also wondering whether the Castle did that to stop this four-hundred-year-old war."

"What difference does that make?"

"It just . . . I always thought that the Castle . . . liked *us* best," Rolf said, and despite the lines the fire put in his face, he sounded younger than Celie. "But maybe nothing it's doing is because of us, maybe it's all still because of *them*."

He gestured as though to encompass the village by the shore, Wizard Bratsch, and the rest of the Glorious Arkower, or Hatheland, or whatever it was called.

Celie shifted around a bit and Rufus clacked his beak sleepily. She'd never thought of that. The Castle always did things for her and her family. When the Castle had started behaving strangely a few months ago, Celie had been disturbed at the thought that the Castle was stealing someone else's feasts and giving them to her family. But even more unsettling was the idea that the Castle wasn't doing any of it out of love for her family, but rather because it wanted them to solve other problems, problems that they didn't even know about.

Neither of them said anything for a while, then Celie kicked at Rolf.

"Don't you dare go to sleep and leave me to think about that alone," she hissed.

"I'm not asleep," Rolf protested, sounding as though that was only half-true.

"You both need to go to sleep," Pogue muttered. "So I can."

"There's not really anyone left here," Celie pointed out. "So I don't think it's doing anything for them anymore. Who's 'them,' anyway? The Arkower?"

"True," Rolf said.

"I thought that Rufus's father would bring the others, but it's been hours. We should go find them," Celie said. She sighed and got to her feet. "Ugh, the lantern's too smoky."

Rolf groaned and creaked as he also stood. He leaned against a windowsill, and suddenly he swore. "That smoke isn't coming from the lantern," he said in alarm.

Screams shattered the air.

"That's Lilah," Pogue said.

Another scream was carried to their ears by the smoke-scented wind.

"That's Lilah all right," Celie said.

"Go to her," Pogue said.

Celie yanked Rufus to his feet and jumped onto his back. The griffin backed away from the window, balking and squawking. Lilah was making a terrific din, and there was a sudden blaze of light out the window as well.

"Rufus, go!" Celie dug her heels into his sides the way she would to a horse, which Rufus hated, but he just backed up again. "Rufus, now!"

Rufus shook himself as though he was trying to get rid of Celie, and she clung tight to the harness. Then they heard another sound from outside: a griffin's cry, and Rufus leaped forward. He pushed Rolf aside and climbed through the window with Celie clinging to his back, then flung himself off into the strangely bright night.

The forest was on fire.

Chapter 14

Rufus began circling, calling out shrilly to the other griffin. From their left came an answering cry and Celie turned to see Rufus's mother arrowing toward them. She sped past, headed straight for the fire, and Rufus followed. Celie didn't object, because that was where the human screaming was coming from.

The griffins folded their wings and dived into the forest not far from the fire. This made Celie very anxious, but when she saw Lilah she forgot all about the fire. The griffins had landed just a few paces from her sister, who was so disheveled that Celie almost didn't recognize her. Lilah's gown was in tatters, her face smeared with dirt, and her hair was a rat's nest. In her arms she cradled a griffin egg that had cracks running all around its surface.

"Lilah!" Celie had to shout to be heard over her sister's screaming.

"It's hatching!" Lilah shrieked. "What do I do?"

"Put it down!" Celie leaped off Rufus's back. "Let it hatch, then let's get out of here! The forest is on fire!"

"I know!" Lilah half knelt, half fell to the ground, lowering the breaking egg with shaking arms. "The Arkower set it on fire!"

"He . . . what?" Celie's stomach lurched, and she thought she must have misheard.

"He set it on fire when I wouldn't give him the egg," Lilah said breathlessly. "Lulath and I were going to go back, but the Arkower came out of nowhere, and Lulath tried to chase him off and I think he got lost. Then the Arkower started the fire, and Rufus's father came and scooped me up and carried me over the flames, but the egg started to hatch and . . . oh!" Lilah broke off, her face transformed. "Here she is!"

All at once the egg crumbled into tiny bits of shell, revealing the newborn griffin within. Celie couldn't tell if it was male or female, but it was definitely smaller and more delicate than Rufus had been at that age. It was a very pale gold, with wings that were almost cream-colored.

"Isn't she lovely?" Lilah breathed. "I will call her Juliet."

Mewling with hunger, the little griffin stumbled into Lilah's lap. Lilah cradled her delicately, while Celie snuffled away tears at the tender scene and worried about what they would do now.

They had two newly hatched griffins to care for (if they

ever found Lulath) and the fire was headed toward them. A smoke-clogged wind was blowing right in Celie's face, carrying the crack and roar of burning trees with it. Celie could see the flames through the trees around them now.

"Lilah, we have to go!"

Celie urged her sister to her feet. Rufus and his mother hovered around them, making cooing noises at the baby. Celie steered Lilah toward Rufus's mother, hoping that she would cooperate. She seemed wilder than her mate . . . and where was he now?

Lady Griffin, as Celie thought of her, did not seem concerned, however. Nor did she seem reluctant to have a rider. She dipped her wing so that Lilah could slither onto her back, sidesaddle, with baby Juliet cuddled to her ruined bodice. Celie showed her sister how to grip the scruff of the griffin's neck where the feathers were short and soft, since Lady Griffin didn't have a harness. Then Celie hurried to get onto Rufus's back. The griffins took off without any urging, but they didn't return to the tower. Instead they circled over the forest, coming ever closer to the smoke and flames.

"Where are we going?" Celie called to Rufus. "We need to get the baby to the tower!" The smoke made her cough, and she yanked weakly at his harness.

Lady Griffin gave a long, low cry, and a griffin within the cover of the trees answered it. Then a figure burst up out of the smoking forest in front of them. It was Rufus's father, and he gave another cry and raced toward them. The other two turned in the air and followed the big male as he made straight for the tower.

✦ ✦ ✦

Celie fell off Rufus's back onto the floor of the tower with great relief, coughing and hacking, her throat and eyes burning with smoke. Lilah slid off more daintily, still holding the crying baby griffin as delicately as if she cradled a breaking egg. Lord Griffin had gotten there first. He inspected Pogue and Rolf with a hard yellow eye and then took up a defensive position in one of the windows.

"Lilah," Rolf said, sounding dumbstruck. "You have a griffin!"

"Isn't she beautiful?" Lilah crouched by the fire. "Is she hungry? Is that why she's crying, Celie?"

"Yes," Celie said. "I just hope we have enough food, even for a very small griffin."

Celie made everyone search their pockets until they located some hard bread to give to Lilah, who fed small pieces to the tiny griffin. Pogue and Rolf admired the little animal while Rufus and Lady Griffin looked on.

Celie longed to inspect the new griffin, but she felt herself drawn to the window instead. She didn't fit beside Lord Griffin, so she took up a position in the window next to his and looked out.

The forest was burning brightly in a great circle some hundred yards beyond the tower. The orange light was vicious, and the smoke was blowing straight at them. As Celie blinked her smoke-reddened eyes, she saw that the fire really was a circle . . . a perfect circle that was getting wider and wider. One edge of the circle was moving along the shore of the poison lake, and it was also coming closer to them.

"Why is the Arkower doing this?" Pogue asked, looking over her shoulder. "He's going to destroy the remains of the Castle and the Builder's tomb!"

"I wouldn't give him the egg," Lilah explained. "He found me in the forest and demanded that I give it to him. I said no, and then it started to hatch. He went mad, shouting that I'd ruined his plans, hundreds of years wasted, and such. I didn't know what to do, so I started to run, then he started the fire, and I just . . . screamed for help." Her face, under its covering of sweat and dirt, glowed red. "The big griffin swooped down and chased the Arkower away, and then you found me, Celie."

"Did he say anything about Lulath? And Lulath's griffin?" Pogue asked.

"He ranted about Rufus and Lorcan, and what a waste it was for Celie and Lulath to have them," Lilah said. "But I don't think he'd captured Lulath. He wasn't *gloating*."

"That's good," Pogue said. He rubbed his face, wincing as his fingers encountered the lump where he'd hit his head.

"Lulath will figure out a way to get back here," Celie said confidently. "He'll probably turn up with Lorcan and a basket of food he's located somewhere." She went to Lilah and stroked Juliet's gold and cream feathers.

Lilah giggled. "That's true." Then her expression clouded over. "The Arkower is insane," she said with a shudder. "We should still look for Lulath, just to make sure he and Lorcan are safe."

"Well, we met our own crazy old wizard in the ruins," Pogue told her. "The last of the Hathelockes, apparently, and he had a great deal to say. We're just trying to piece it all to—Rolf, are you all right?"

Rolf was staring fixedly at the tiny griffin as Lilah continued to feed her whatever scraps of food she could find. He tore his gaze away for a moment, looked at Pogue and then Celie with an anguished expression, then back at little Juliet.

"Ye-es," he said. Then, after a moment, "No, no I'm not!" He drew in a deep breath. "*I* wanted a griffin!"

They all blinked at him.

Rolf's face was red. "I wanted to bring this egg with us . . . well . . . I assumed *I* would bond with it," he said. "Do you have any idea how jealous I've been of Celie since the minute I saw Rufus? I mean, she's already the Castle's favorite, and now it gives her this amazing creature, too?"

Celie shook her head. "You're the next king!" But she couldn't fight the little niggle of pleasure at being called the favorite.

"I'd rather have a griffin," Rolf sulked.

"Oh, Rolf," Lilah said impatiently. "We'll find another egg, and then you'll have your griffin. But for now we have other concerns!"

"You can say that: you have a griffin, and you never even wanted one!" Rolf snapped.

"The first king, the Builder, had a griffin," Celie pointed out by way of making peace. She truly didn't want to be the king—er, queen. "I'm sure the Castle will want you to have one, since you're the next king." She remembered the collar in her pouch. "And Daddy should have one, too, and it should wear the collar." She realized that she was mostly talking to herself, and stopped. When they got home, then they would see what the collar could do. And the crown, and the rings.

"As Lilah said, finding another baby griffin that will need constant feeding is the last thing we need right now," Pogue said, keeping vigil at the window. "The fire is moving closer and we still don't know where Lulath is."

Celie went to stand beside Pogue again, ignoring Rolf, who continued to seethe. The other, still-dead tower had flames licking at its base. They could feel the heat beating on their faces even from this distance, and she felt her stomach tie itself in a knot. Would it hurt the Castle to be engulfed in flames? And what would happen to them? Stone didn't burn, usually, but this was a *wizard* fire.

"All right," Pogue said. "We've got to move. Now. The fire is only getting closer, and I doubt the Arkower will care if we burn up in here."

"I wonder if Bratsch could help us," Celie mused.

"There's no time," Pogue told her, turning away from the window. "And his hut is about to be consumed by the fire as well. I say we get the griffins to take us around the fire to the Tomb of the Builder. I may be wrong, but from here it looks like it's still not touched by the fire."

"Agreed," Rolf said, shaking off his funk. "Everybody on a griffin!"

Celie checked that the ring, crown, and collar were safely fastened in her pouch. She mounted Rufus, and Rolf helped Lilah and Juliet onto Lady Griffin. Both young men looked at each other, then at the large male griffin still standing guard at the window. Pogue opened his mouth but it was Rolf who spoke first.

"Excuse me, sir," he said politely, and gave a little bow. The griffin turned his head slightly to look at him with one eye. "We really must get ourselves and this baby griffin to safety. Would you be so kind as to carry my friend and myself to the tomb of the first king? The Builder?"

The griffin king studied him for another moment, then turned back to the window. Rolf's shoulders started to slump, but the griffin tucked his wings and dipped a knee to make it easier for them to mount.

"Sir, we thank you," Rolf said.

He mounted, and Pogue after him. The big griffin led the way, leaping out of the tower and over the lake rather than the forest, which blazed angrily.

"Why is the Arkower doing this?" Celie muttered. "Why now? After all these years of not imprinting a griffin, why doesn't he just give up?"

Rufus carked in reply, sounding equally baffled, and

then it hit Celie. The Arkower had always wanted a griffin, wanted them for all his people. He'd practically destroyed his entire world to get one. And then Celie came, with Rufus. Rufus, who was devoted to her, and she to him, and proved that it could still be done. That even someone who'd never seen a griffin before could ride one. Oh, how that must sting! Celie thought. No wonder he was willing to burn down the forest to get to them! She felt a surge of terror and knew that they had to get away from Hatheland or the Glorious Arkower or whatever this place was, and fast.

Rufus flew wide over the lake, and in the orange glow of the fire Celie looked down over his shoulder at the peaceful cauldron of poison. She could not imagine hating anyone so strongly that you were willing to kill thousands of people and animals to rid yourself of your enemy. But then, the Arkower had had many centuries to develop his hatred of the Hathelockes.

They finally flew past the edge of the fire and landed in the little clearing where they had first found the map on the back of Lilah's cape. It seemed like weeks ago, but Celie realized with a shock that it was . . . the day before. Two days ago? With another shock she discovered that she honestly didn't remember. Not only that, she couldn't remember the last time she had eaten, and she was so tired that she fell trying to get off Rufus's back, and landed atop her makeshift pack with a whoosh of air.

"All right?" Rolf hurried over to help her up.

"Yes," Celie gasped, winded.

Pogue helped Lilah down from Lady Griffin, then looked around. "We all need some sleep. Should we go into the mound?"

"And sleep in a tomb?" Lilah's voice cracked. Juliet was crying with hunger again, and Lilah looked strained.

"We really don't have much choice, I'm afraid," Rolf said. "I was just going to suggest it myself. Halfway underground, it's probably the safest place to be."

"The tomb is being nice, but in the tunnel is also having some rooms," Lulath said, striding into the clearing with Lorcan still peeping out of the front of his ragged tunic. "Oh, my our dear Lilah! You are also having a fine griffin darling! What joy!"

The griffins broke into cries of welcome, while Celie was embarrassed to find tears of relief coursing down her cheeks. Pogue and Rolf could only gape, and Lilah, too, was in tears. Then she screamed and threw her arms around Lulath in an awkward embrace with the griffins squashed between them.

"You're alive, you're alive," Lilah sobbed into Lulath's ruined tunic.

"Come along," Lulath said, patting her back tenderly. "Not the tears now! Into this tunnel we will be having a go!"

Chapter
15

Celie and Lilah and the others were all still trying to cry and laugh and hug Lulath and his griffin at once, but the tall prince was having none of it. He herded them around the mound to the entrance, griffins and all, nodding and smiling at their excited chatter.

"Yes, it is all so very," he said. "But we are going in the tunnel now, and talking later."

"What tunnel?" Pogue wanted to know.

"It is being a fine tunnel that I am finding in the nearness to the first king's place of final sleeping," Lulath explained. "Come, only through seeing is there to be belief!"

As they followed him, Celie realized that they had five griffins with them. They would soon be able to fill the griffin stable back at the Castle.

If they ever got back.

"I am not knowing how far it is delving into this earth,"

Lulath said, approaching the entrance and easily pulling open the door. "But we are being very safe from the fire."

They crowded into the Tomb of the Builder, which was even more brightly lit than before. Every torch blazed and threw long shadows around the dome-shaped chamber. Celie tried not to step on something, and to keep Rufus under control, as they crossed to where the king and his griffin were laid out on their biers.

"It is being hidden just here, beside the noble of kings," Lulath said.

The griffins moved easily through the baskets and boxes and statues, as though they knew the way. Celie worried that the sight of the ancient griffin's body would upset them, and took a firmer hold on Rufus. But Lord Griffin merely looked with interest at both king and beast, and then turned away. Lady Griffin ignored the area entirely, and Rufus seemed to take his cue from her.

"There is being a ring of the iron here, for opening," Lulath said, squatting down at the head of the Builder's bier. Lorcan almost fell out of his tunic, and Lulath shoved him back in with one hand. The prince grunted, shifting the heavy stone.

"How did you find this?" Rolf asked.

"Here I came to hide from that wizard, who I think is not being evil but also sick in the head," Lulath told them. "Also, perhaps being just too old." Lulath nodded thoughtfully. "And my Lorcan, he is sniffing about for the food, and finding this ring, and I am saying, what could this be? So strange! Let me be looking, and behold, a tunnel!" He gave them a triumphant look as a final tug revealed a square opening and stone steps winding away into the darkness beneath the mound.

"There is being lamps, but I did put them out, for the fire safeness," Lulath told them. "Friend Pogue, if you will be that torch bringing."

Celie turned to watch as Pogue got a torch, and saw something on the wall that gave her pause. Between two of the torch holders there was a little wooden shelf that had been bolted to the wall. There was a cushion on the shelf, but nothing else. She frowned. The cushion was pale green and had a dent in it that was shaped like a crescent, and reminded her of something.

"What do you suppose that is?" Lilah had followed her gaze. "It doesn't seem to go here, does it?"

"We know that someone besides us robbed the tomb," Rolf remarked. He, too, had gotten a torch off the wall. "Not just Ethan, I mean, but even before that."

"I don't think so," Celie said. "Ethan was too upset by what the Arkower made him do, and I don't think anyone else has been inside. So the only thing that's been taken is the broken piece of the Eye.

"Or at least, that's what Wizard Bratsch says."

"Who is he being when he is being in his home?" Lulath asked. He was holding out a hand to Lilah, to help her down the steps.

"The opposite of the Arkower," Pogue said. "They're

157

apparently mortal enemies, but both of them are lying about something, so I'm not sure Bratsch is on our side, either."

"There is something I can't put my finger on," Celie muttered, still staring at the cushion. "If that's the shape of the piece of the Eye, it's not very big . . ."

"Come on, Cel, let's see what this tunnel is like," Rolf said, taking her arm.

The stone steps wound around in a half turn and ended on a hard-packed dirt floor. Lulath hurried to light the lamps, casting a warm glow ahead of them down the dark corridor. The whole tunnel was dirt, with wooden beams to shore it up.

"How long is it?" Celie asked as Lulath joined her.

"I am not finding the end," Lulath said. "Not as yet. But it is in the direction of, and of such length, that it is seeming possible to reach the Castle ruins."

Lord Griffin, who had come down the stairs after Lulath, pushed his way to the front again. With a hoarse cry that seemed to say that they should follow him, he started down the tunnel. Celie looked at Lulath, who shrugged, so they followed. After a while, they found some lamps that Lulath hadn't lit, and Pogue hurried to light them. Ever capable, he'd also pulled the tunnel entrance closed after they'd all entered.

Just as the new baby griffins were starting to cry again from hunger, the tunnel bulged out into a decent-size room. It even had a few chairs, and more beams and lamps. Pogue lit the lamps, and Lilah sank into one of the chairs with a sigh that ruffled the feathers of Juliet's sleek head.

Celie collapsed onto the hard floor, and Rufus quickly lay down behind her to support her back. She threw an arm around him in gratitude. She was so tired, but she didn't want to fall asleep and miss anything. Her eyes drifted down just for a second, and when she opened them again, the others were gathered around Lulath.

". . . which of course I am thinking was done only that my Lorcan might leave freely with me," Lulath was saying as Celie opened her eyes again.

"Amazing," Rolf said. "Such clever creatures." The envy was plain in his voice.

"Who did what?" Celie's voice was little more than a croak.

"Cel! Are you awake?" Rolf hurried to her side. "You've been snoring!"

Celie felt herself blushing a deep red.

"Rolf! You don't need to tell her that," Lilah scolded him. She brought Celie a waterskin, and Celie drank the luke-warm water greedily.

"Well, you were," Rolf said with a grin. He offered her some cheese and a round biscuit, and she snatched them from his hands and shoved them both into her mouth at the same time.

"Where did you get the food?" She could hardly talk again, but this time it was because her mouth was full.

"Lulath," Rolf said simply.

"Oh, I missed his story," Celie lamented after she swallowed. Then she took another biscuit and chunk of cheese.

"It is being as a nothing," Lulath called over to her. "I am only sitting and feeding my little Lorcan, after our Rolf and our Pogue are flying away, and feeding him and feeding him. Then to myself I think, I must be saving of the food, so that when we are again together, we could be having some." He shrugged. "And saying also, that I am not knowing where the Ethan is."

"Oh, dear," Celie said.

"He went back to his master, didn't he?" Pogue asked. He made a disgusted face and kicked at the packed dirt of the wall.

"Of a sureness no," Lulath said, shaking his head emphatically. "Before the Arkower is coming to shout and wave the arms at me, the Ethan is saying to me that there is a thing in this forest which he must do. Or see. Bring?" Lulath frowned. "I am not remembering, but it was not a thing that the Arkower is telling to him to be doing."

"I wonder what he has to do that's so urgent?" Pogue still sounded suspicious. "Well, is everyone rested? I'd like to go farther along the tunnel and see what's what." He was pacing rapidly around the small chamber, showing no signs of having rested himself, despite the fatigue evidenced by the dark circles under his eyes. "We don't know what's happening up there, and it's making me twitchy."

Rolf went over and looked down the tunnel toward the

Castle ruins. Or in the direction that they hoped led to the Castle ruins, anyway.

"I am agreeing with you, Friend Pogue," Lulath said. He gathered up his things and popped Lorcan back into his tunic. "We must be finding the way back to Sleyne! I am thinking it will be of greater ease now, when there is only small griffins and not eggs to carry."

"We'll see," Pogue said, not looking convinced. "Celie, are you up for more walking?"

"Yes, I'm fine!"

She tried to leap to her feet, embarrassed that they all seemed to be waiting for her. But her body wouldn't leap, and instead she fell over sideways.

"Are you all right?" Lilah scrambled to try to help her, but Juliet got entangled in Lilah's skirts, and Lilah nearly fell on top of Celie.

Pogue leaned down and picked Celie up, setting her on her feet with a small smile. "Tired?"

"So tired," Celie agreed.

"We'll be home soon," Pogue told her with perfect certainty.

"Let's get back to the ruins," Rolf said. "We need to see how far that fire has spread, and what the Arkower is going to do next." His face was grim.

"You certainly perked up," Lilah said to him, gathering Juliet into her arms. "A moment ago you were too busy pouting over not having a griffin to care about getting back."

"There's something down here," Rolf said, pointing

down the tunnel. "Can't you feel it?" He rolled his head around, stretching his neck. "We really need to see where this leads.

"Cel, why don't I carry the crown and ring?" He held out his hand for the pouch.

Celie blinked at him. None of them had cared who carried the crown before, and it certainly wasn't heavy, but she supposed there was no reason why Rolf couldn't have it. Still, she hesitated.

"It's fine," she said. "It's not heavy."

"Just let me carry them for a while," Rolf said.

Celie thought of her secret dream of presenting their father with the crown and ring. She put a hand over the bag.

"Celie, I need them," Rolf said, looking at her intently. "I need them."

She was too tired, and Rolf was too insistent. Slowly she handed him the pouch, he fastened it to his own waist, and she breathed a little resigned sigh.

Pogue picked Celie up again and put her on Rufus's back. Celie would have felt embarrassed at being treated like a child, but she was just too tired. She felt as though she was drowning in honey, every movement too slow and deliberate. She worried that Rufus was too tired to carry her, but he didn't seem to mind, so she stuck her hands under the straps of his harness and let her shoulders slump.

"Lead on, our Rolf," Lulath said cheerily.

Rolf started down the tunnel without even looking

around. The others followed at a more sedate pace, stopping to light the lamps as they went. Rolf went on into the darkness, oblivious, and the full-grown griffins followed at his heels, seeming to be bothered by the light.

"This is worrisome," Pogue remarked as he lit another lamp.

Celie, sitting on Rufus nearby, didn't answer. Rolf's behavior was worrying her, too. He was moving out of sight, marching along as though he knew exactly where he was going, and no amount of calling had brought him back. He hadn't even turned his head the last time Pogue had shouted his name.

"Be not afraid," Lulath said. "It is my only thinking that the Castle has our Rolf in its grip. This is being not such a bad thing."

"Lulath," Lilah said with exasperation as they moved on to the next lamp. "Doesn't *anything* ever bother you?"

"Yes," Lulath said, his voice curt for the first time in Celie's memory of the Grathian prince. "Of course! I am telling this of our Celie only the yesterday! But we are all needing our shoes on but one at a time, and going forward!"

Lilah made a small noise and subsided.

"Lulath," Celie said, startled out of her exhaustion for a moment. "Goodness!"

Lulath froze in his tracks. "Oh, it was being so rude! Oh, our Lilah, can you be forgiving of this man?" He looked for a moment like he was going to throw himself at Lilah's feet.

"It is being so horrible here," he babbled. "And the Lorcan, I am wanting for him only good things, but this tunnel it only goes on and the fire and the Arkower . . ."

"It's all right," Lilah said in a husky voice, reaching out to stop Lulath from flinging himself around and endangering Lorcan. "I understand."

"Do you think they're going to start kissing?" Celie whispered to Pogue.

Pogue sighed. "We need to catch Rolf," he announced. "Come along, all of you." And he marched ahead.

Celie blinked. "What's wrong with *him* now?" she asked Rufus. Then she remembered that Pogue used to come to the Castle every day to see Lilah . . . something that had stopped in the last few months, when Lilah had started spending much more time with Lulath. "Oh," she said, feeling foolish.

"Where is that light coming from?" Lilah said, turning away from Lulath. "Do you see it?"

"I see it," Celie said in a hushed voice.

Up ahead, Rolf was illuminated by a light shining toward them from the opposite end of the tunnel. It was a hazy, orange light, like a lantern, and Celie felt her breath catch in her chest. Was it the Arkower?

Pogue rushed forward to stand beside Rolf, and the adult griffins flanked them. They were packed so tightly in the tunnel now that Celie worried they wouldn't have room to maneuver if it came to a fight. Lulath moved to stand beside her, holding little Lorcan tight to his chest with one hand, and resting his other lightly on Celie's shoulder.

"Be ready to have the Rufus turning and have him on the run," Lulath whispered to her. "Lilah?" he called in a slightly louder whisper. "You will be ready for running, please."

"I am," Lilah whispered, her face drawn and chalky in the lamplight.

The light grew brighter, spilling past Rolf and Pogue and the large griffins until it reached Celie and Rufus. She blinked in the brightness, and when her eyes cleared she saw a little man holding a dusty lantern high in one gnarled hand.

"Are you coming?" Wizard Bratsch asked sharply. "We haven't much time."

Chapter
16

⟨❦⟩

Who is that?" Lilah said in a cracked whisper.

"Wizard Bratsch. He's the Hathelocke wizard we told you about," Celie said. "The opposite of the Arkower."

"I see," Lilah said, but she still sounded worried. "Can he help us?"

"We can hope," Celie said.

She still didn't know how to feel about the Hathelocke wizard's revelations. Just trying to sort out what was truth and what was lies in anything they knew about the Castle's history made her feel even more tired. If only there was some rule that wizards couldn't lie. But she supposed that everyone had to lie sometime.

"I am not thinking that I will take a like to him," Lulath announced. It was almost as shocking as his revelation about being afraid. "He is strange around the eyes."

Celie studied Wizard Bratsch's eyes in the lantern light.

They looked like they were the same faded noncolor that they'd been before. Well, you could see the whites all the way around, and he didn't really look at you when you were talking to him, but he was very old, after all.

"Let's go," Rolf called over his shoulder.

Wizard Bratsch turned and led them back the way he'd come, holding the lantern in one shaking hand. Rolf followed so close behind him that Celie was afraid Rolf would step on the elderly wizard, and Pogue kept close behind Rolf with an adult griffin on either side.

"I am having the bad feelings about this," Lulath said.

"He's just really old," Celie said uneasily.

"I heard that," Wizard Bratsch called back. He was grinning at Celie over his shoulder. "I've got life in me yet!"

The grin made her fully agree with Lulath. There was something *off* about Wizard Bratsch, but she really didn't know how else to describe it, or why.

Or what choice they had but to keep following him.

The tunnel was sloping upward, and the light was growing brighter. At last they emerged from the tunnel, coming out in the shelter of a half-collapsed corner of the griffin stable. In front of them spread the broken, weed-choked stones of the ruined courtyard leading to the hatching tower Celie had brought back to life.

Which was now engulfed in flames.

The entire forest around the ruins seemed to be on fire. Celie could feel the waves of heat even from where she stood. Rufus raised his wings and screamed at the licking orange tongues of flame as they ran up the walls of the towers and consumed the trees.

"What do we do?"

Celie looked frantically from Lilah to Lulath to Pogue. They were all frozen with matching expressions of horror on their faces. She looked around for Rolf, but he was still walking without looking back, just as he had done in the tunnel.

"Rolf," Celie yelled. "What are you doing?"

Her brother was moving across the broken courtyard with long, purposeful strides, his head held high. He was walking straight toward the living hatching tower, seemingly oblivious to the fire and smoke.

And the Arkower.

The Arkower was standing at the other side of the courtyard, also without appearing to notice the flames. He was waving his arms over his head and shouting in a strange language, and Celie wasn't sure if he was shouting insults at them, or if it was all part of his fire spell. She heartily wished that Bran were there to help them, not only with the Arkower, but just . . . to help them.

Rolf stopped in the center of the courtyard.

Celie thought that maybe he was going to shout back at the Arkower, but Rolf wasn't even facing the old wizard. He was looking somewhere between the tower and the burning forest, his back to Celie and the others, and yet somehow she knew that he wasn't seeing what was in front of him, either.

Wizard Bratsch, who Celie had forgotten was even there, suddenly cried out in his ancient, cracked voice. "Do it, boy! Do it now!"

Perhaps Rolf heard him, perhaps he was just moving with the prompting of the Castle, but he knelt down in the middle of the courtyard, and bowed his head. He took out the crown and placed it gently atop his head, and then slipped the ring onto his right hand, casting the pouch aside.

Celie was sure now that the Castle was directing Rolf. She slid off Rufus's back and walked forward a few steps, wanting to go to Rolf but also afraid of interrupting him. Then she remembered the collar in the pouch, and ran forward to snatch it up, tying it to her sash again.

Rolf brought his arms out, clenched his fists, and then punched the broken cobbles so hard that Celie cried out, afraid he would break both his hands. A ripple ran across the courtyard. Celie could see it and feel it, and she let out a little shriek when it reached her feet. Lilah shrieked, too, as the stones beneath them buckled . . . and healed.

The broken stone right in front of Celie shivered and then the two halves sealed back together as though they had never been cracked. The crumbling edges smoothed out, fitting themselves snugly against the neighboring stones, which were also now smooth and without crack or chip.

The ripple had run out in all directions, as though Rolf were a stone thrown into a still pond. When it hit the other tower, the one Celie could not awaken, it surged up, every stone shivering and then falling back into place, new and whole and clean. The tower that she'd already awakened didn't seem to be affected, but it was also completely engulfed in flames.

"I wonder if water will put it out," Celie said.

"What?" Pogue looked at her, distracted.

"The fire," Celie said. "I wonder if water will put out a wizard fire."

"I hope so," Pogue said. "Otherwise I don't know what we'll do."

"How could we possibly put out a fire that big?" Lilah looked half-wild. "I say we run for it."

"Where?" Celie asked simply. "Where would we run?"

"Home," Lilah said fervidly. "Now that these ruins are awake . . . Can't we go home and just leave all this?" She made a gesture that included the wizards and the fire.

Celie's heart leaped. They could. They could go home. Maybe this was the Castle's way of bringing them home. But the ripple had passed and Rolf was walking back toward them now, looking dazed, and they still hadn't been pulled back to Sleyne.

And the forest was on fire. And by now the village was, too. And the Arkower was still shouting, and they had yet to find the missing piece of the Eye.

"We are going to need a lot of water," Celie announced.

"How . . . we don't even have buckets . . . there's not even a well," Lilah protested.

"We have griffins," Celie reminded her. "And there are buckets in this very stable."

She moved to the door of the stable and went in. There they were, just as she'd remembered: a pile of buckets that had probably been used to carry feed. Celie picked up a stack and brought them back out to the courtyard just as Rolf reached them.

"We need to bring water from the stream to put out the fire," Celie told him.

Rolf blinked stupidly at her. The crown had slipped down onto his brows and he looked very young and very tired. "We need to find the Eye," he said.

"We need to get out of here before we all die," Lilah interjected.

"We can't let the Castle be destroyed," Celie argued. "Even this little piece of it. Or the wild griffins in the . . ." A light dawned. She turned sharply and faced Lord Griffin. "We need water," she said slowly. "Water for the fire." She pointed to it, then held out a bucket. "Water, for the fire. Tell the other griffins. Bring more griffins."

"Celie, they don't understand," Rolf began.

Lord Griffin gave an earsplitting scream that made the Arkower pause in his shouting, and then he leaped into the air. Celie turned to Lady Griffin and Rufus and gave them each a bucket.

"Bring water," she ordered. "Water."

They each grasped a bucket in their beak and then followed Lord Griffin into the sky.

"Are they really going to do it?" Rolf's voice was hushed.

"We can only hope," Pogue said.

171

"But of a surety," Lulath said. "It is the Celie asking, and who is not loving the Celie?" He beamed at her.

Celie blushed. "Well, if you speak slowly and look into their eyes, the griffins seem to understand quite a lot . . . We'll just keep our fingers crossed."

The fire was starting to slither around the edges of the newly restored courtyard. Celie sent up a silent prayer that Lord Griffin really had understood.

"What have you done?"

It took them all a moment to realize that the Arkower was addressing them now. He'd been standing to the side ranting for so long that Celie had forgotten that he could actually see them. Now he came storming across the court-yard, robes flapping and face dark with rage.

"*What have you done?*" The Arkower stomped his foot on the smooth paving stones, looking wild-eyed. "The Castle will ruin everything now! It's been corrupted by the Hathe-locke filth!"

"What have *we* done?" Celie surprised herself by scream-ing back at him. "*You've* lit the entire forest on fire, and now the towers are aflame!"

"To get rid of you!" the Arkower shouted at her. "To drive you out so that I may regain my Castle!"

"*We* built the Castle!" Wizard Bratsch howled at him. "It's you who tried to subvert it! Who twisted it and broke it!"

"You didn't build the Castle," the Arkower countered. "Your long-dead king, the only one of you worth my spit, built it to be a safe haven for all who wished!"

"The griffins choose their riders, and they would never choose you, you vile coward!" Wizard Bratsch spit as he screamed the words, his gaunt form trembling like an autumn leaf.

"Nor would they choose you! They saw you for what you are!" the Arkower shouted back.

"This is awful," Lilah whispered. "Should we leave? I always thought that wizards were supposed to be noble and dignified . . . self-sacrificing! Not like this."

"Yes," Lulath said in a hushed voice. "This is not being noble, this is being madness."

"They've been here alone so long," Rolf agreed. "Their obsession with the Castle and the griffins has driven them mad."

"Well!" Celie started to shout at the wizards again, then changed her mind. "We don't have time for this!" She turned and started back into the stable.

"Actually, this interests me," she heard Pogue say as she went. "Maybe now we'll hear the truth."

He was right, but the Castle was still on fire. She couldn't stand there and watch two mad old men screech like birds after the same worm. Her feet itched, she was so anxious to do *something*.

She moved farther into the stable, looking for more buckets. There were a lot of oddments in the corners of the stalls. Rufus liked to hoard things as well, and Celie had a pang of homesickness as she thought of the piles of toys in the corners of his tower back at the Castle. He occasionally stole shoes and added them, and once one of Celie's favorite bracelets. She patted the lump in her bodice where Rufus the lion resided, and wondered what other treasures Lord and Lady Griffin might have collected over the years. Her feet twinged almost painfully, and she worried that she'd picked up lice or fleas.

"Buckets," she reminded herself aloud. "We need buckets."

She scuffed aside branches and bits of old furniture, a bronze arm from a statue that gave her a start because it looked so lifelike, and the chunk of thick, grime-coated glass that she had stepped on when she'd found her toy. She shoved it aside with one foot, and the itching became almost unbearable.

Behind the debris she found a bucket and grabbed it up eagerly, but it had a large hole in the bottom. There was a familiar twist in her head that meant the Castle had moved, and the broad stones rippled. Celie looked around but didn't see anything different. Then she heard shouting—different from the wizards' continued argument—and hurried out of the stable to look.

"More griffins are coming," Rolf shouted to her, pointing up at the sky.

Golden figures filled the sky, swooping down over the angry red fire. They dived at the buckets that Celie had already found, laid out in neat rows now by a nervous Rolf, snatching them up in their talons and soaring back into the sky, where they circled over the courtyard.

Lord Griffin, his form almost as familiar now as Rufus's,

flew over one of the towers and upended a bucket of water on the flames, then flew off with a scream of triumph. His mate followed, then Rufus, leaving gouts of steam in their wake. The other griffins were quick to follow them away, no doubt to fill their buckets.

"They keep coming," Rolf said in awe.

"We're going to need more buckets," Pogue said.

"I found one more, but it's got a hole," Celie said.

"Show me," Pogue said. "I might be able to fix it."

Rolf followed them into the stable and began to look at the other stalls, while Pogue followed Celie down to the end. She picked up the bucket and showed it to him, then kicked around again to see if there was another one hidden anywhere. Her toe connected with the chunk of glass and it skittered away under some dry branches. Her whole foot tingled and the floor rippled.

"What was that?" Rolf called down the aisle.

"Nothing," Pogue said. "I didn't say anything, did you?" Baffled, he looked at Celie and shrugged before he turned back to the bucket. "If I had a piece of leather I could get this to hold water, but it's probably not worth it."

Celie made a noncommittal noise. She was trying to find that chunk of glass. She finally located it, hidden by stale straw and wedged under the wooden partition between two of the stalls. When she reached down and put her fingertips on it, trying to pry it loose, her fingers began to itch and the floor shuddered.

"All right, what was *that?*" Rolf demanded.

"What was what?" Pogue asked. He moved on to another stall, setting the broken bucket on a shelf. "I have no idea what you're talking about."

Celie pulled the glass free and held it up to the dim light coming from the open door. Only now that she was really looking at it, she could see that it wasn't glass. Underneath the grime there were facets and flickers. This was a gemstone, and a big one: curved like a crescent moon, as big as her fist, and with a jagged break across one side and a bit of tarnished gold set on the other. She sighed with relief as the itching in her hands and feet stopped.

"What've you got, Cel?" Rolf called over to her.

"Oh, nothing," she said, trying to sound casual despite the tremor in her voice. "Only the missing piece of the Eye of the Castle."

Chapter
17

⁓⧤⧥⁓

When they stumbled out of the stable, with Celie cradling the pale green stone against her chest and Rolf and Pogue at her shoulders like an honor guard, they saw a continuous line of griffins sailing over the fire, dumping buckets of water, and then wheeling away again. Most of the griffins were smaller and brownish: the wild griffins like those Celie had seen being chased into the forest before. But a few of them were proud golden creatures, screaming battle cries and often carrying a bucket in each foreclaw.

The wizards had stopped shouting, but they were locked in some sort of silent magical struggle, their faces strained and their fists clenched, their eyes fixed on each other with an intensity that made Celie wonder if one or both of them would suddenly burst into flame. She tried to cover the Eye completely with her fingers and turned away to quietly show the others.

"Your hands are filthy!" Lilah wrinkled her nose. "What is that?"

"It's the Eye," Celie told her. "I feel so stupid! I actually stepped on it before, when I met Rufus's parents, but I didn't know what it was!"

"You couldn't have known," Pogue assured her.

"The Eye? You found it?" Lilah grabbed Celie's shoulders and shook her in delight. "You clever girl!"

Rolf tried to shush her, but it was too late. Despite the intensity of his silent battle with Wizard Bratsch, the Arkower spared them a glance, and his face turned the color of whey. At his rival's change of expression, Bratsch turned and then he, too, paled.

"I thought it was finally gone," he said in a hoarse whisper.

"What?" Celie took a step back, nearly tripping over Rolf, who steadied her with a hand on each shoulder.

"Easy," Rolf whispered in her ear.

"I knew it," Pogue said softly from the other side. "They're both guilty."

"Once it was broken I tried to destroy the piece we kept back," Bratsch repeated. "But even my magic was not great enough, so I hid it away. And then it was lost . . . I wanted it to be finally gone."

"Your hiding place wasn't very clever, was it?" the Arkower jeered.

"You took it!" Bratsch pointed a shaking finger at his rival. "You defiled the tomb of my ancestor!"

"You defiled his very name when you broke the treaty," the Arkower snapped back.

"What treaty?" Rolf asked, his fingers tightening on Celie's shoulders as both wizards turned to glare at them.

Celie got ready to turn, but to her surprise the Arkower answered them, seething with rage. He took a step toward them, and as a body they all took a step back. From above, one of the griffins screamed a warning.

"The Hathelockes wanted their Castle back," he sneered. "They were living in the mountain with their griffins. We wanted griffins, but we deserved the Castle, too. So we made a treaty. All those who were accepted by the griffins could live in the Castle, and the Hathelockes would allow the griffins to choose from among Arkish children as well." His face darkened again. "But they didn't give us the griffins we wanted, and—"

"They would not accept you!" Bratsch looked as though he might strike the Arkower. "For years we tried, but they looked into your hearts and knew that you were rotten!"

"None would accept you, either," the Arkower raged back. "Oath-breaker! You are a shame and an embarrassment to the Castle and your people! Say what you will about the Arkish, but we kept our promises!"

"I would not see my Castle and my heritage befouled by you all," Bratsch ranted. "If I had to hide a hundred eggs from your kind or poison a thousand lakes, I would!"

Celie gasped. "It was you, wasn't it?" She felt sick. "You poisoned the lake and the griffins, not him!"

"We both did," Bratsch said, sounding like a whining child trying to avoid punishment.

"I caught him at it," the Arkower said, sounding equally childish. "I caught him poisoning the lake, and he said that it would only make the riders sick, not the griffins. I agreed to keep it up, to help, thinking that if the Hathelockes were gone, there would be a greater chance for the Arkish to become griffin riders."

"You're both so *evil*," Rolf said.

"Don't be so high and mighty," snapped Bratsch. "You wouldn't have that pretty little crown, or the right to wear it, if it weren't for me. I decided to send the Castle away with the remaining riders, and I decided to send it to your precious Sleyne, too." He pointed a shaking hand at the Arkower. "And that creature is the one who broke the Eye and crippled the Castle."

"To keep it away from here, and away from you," the Arkower said. "And I have no regrets!"

"Then why did you steal the shard?" Bratsch demanded. "It rested safe in the Builder's tomb for hundreds of years. Why did you take it?"

The Arkower's face contorted. He looked as though he was going to swallow his tongue, and Celie got ready to slip away, figuring that they wouldn't get any more truth out of the wizards right now.

"He tried to bring the griffins," called a rough voice over the roar of the fire.

They all twisted around, looking for the source of the

voice. A figure, soot-blackened, coughing, was emerging from the edge of the forest. Lord Griffin dropped his bucket and flew down to stand beside Celie and Rolf, taking up a defensive position. The strange figure had almost reached them when Celie realized that it was Ethan.

"He promised us griffins," Ethan said, stopping just out of reach of both parties. "All the young men. Said we would get back the Castle, when we had griffins." He bent over, rested his hands on his knees, and coughed for a moment. "He took the shard," Ethan went on, his voice raw from breathing smoke. He pointed to the Arkower. "He tried to attract the griffins with it, royal griffins, but the only one we ever saw was that one." He waved a hand at Lord Griffin. "And it just took the shard and flew away."

"Good boy," Rolf said, and reached out to thump Lord Griffin on the flank.

The king of the griffins gave him a patient look and didn't move away.

"When he hid it in the stable, that must have been what sent the Castle into confusion," Celie said.

"Which is why we must get it and the crown and ring away from here now," Bratsch said, holding out a hand. "Now. Now. Give it to me now."

Celie backed away from him, taking Rolf with her.

"You? Mad old monster," the Arkower said. "Give the things to me, children, and I will take care of them." He, too, held out a hand.

"First stop this fire," Pogue said. "Then we'll talk."

181

"Tell your servant not to address a wizard," Bratsch said to Rolf. "There's no stopping a wizard fire once it gets started."

"Did you start this?" Lilah demanded.

"Of course not, but I won't try to stop it," Bratsch said. "It's better this way."

"How is this being better?" Lulath wanted to know.

He had one arm around Lilah, and was also guiding her backward. If they went any farther, they would wind up inside the stable. Now that Rolf had awoken it, the broken back wall had healed, and there was no way to escape the low building. Celie wondered if they should duck back through the tunnel, but the wizards were both quite spry, in spite of being so old.

Rolf reached up and adjusted the crown.

"No one is taking anything from us," he said in a voice that sounded like their father's. "We are taking all this"— he swept out an arm to indicate the courtyard, the towers, and even the griffins—"back to Sleyne. Right now." He looked down at Celie. "Ready, Cel?"

Celie nodded, trying to summon her own courage. She gripped the shard of the Eye in both hands and held it up in front her. Lord Griffin caught her eye, and she nodded at him. He let out a cry so loud and commanding that it scared them all, and the baby griffins started to mewl.

The wizards both raised their voices to argue, but were drowned out by the cries of the fleet of griffins that now came winging toward their king. Many of them still carried full buckets, and as Rufus came in for a landing he dropped his. It cracked open and the water splashed across Celie and Rolf, soaking them both.

"Hey, that burns," Rolf yelled, his dignity forgotten.

"Rufus," Celie said as the water sizzled through the rips in her sleeves and she felt the skin on her arms blister. "Where did you get that water?"

Chapter 18

⁓

When Celie spoke, some of the water that had splashed her face ran into her mouth and she began to gasp and choke. It tasted vile, and she fought the urge to vomit as it hit her stomach. She looked down and saw to her horror that the skin on the backs of her hands was blistering as though burned, even though the water was icy cold.

"The lake," she choked out. "The plague."

"No!" Lilah screamed. "One of you *do* something!" She leaped at the wizards, nearly dropping Juliet in her panic, but Lulath grabbed her before she reached them.

The two old men had drawn back, away from Celie and Rolf and the wet stones around them, and once more their ire had turned them on each other.

"You said I would have griffins, griffins to command," the Arkower raged.

"You said I would control the Castle, I alone!" Bratsch screamed back.

"You're both horrible and I hope you die here!" Lilah's voice rose over the shouting wizards and the distressed cries of her little griffin, clutched to her bodice.

Celie felt dizzy. She put her hand to the bodice of her own gown, feeling the lump of Rufus the lion there. She leaned against Rufus the griffin, having a sudden strong memory of standing on the battlements with Khelsh, all the shouting, the threats, the blood dripping down her arm . . .

She looked at her finger, where there was a deep cut from the crown, now stinging two times over as the cursed lake water seeped into the wound.

"Pogue," she gasped.

"Are you dying?" Pogue reached for her and Celie pulled away just in time. She was soaked with poison, and she didn't want anyone else to get the plague.

"Rufus," she croaked, realizing too late that her darling griffin was thoroughly wetted as well.

He shook his head as though a fly were buzzing around him, and made a strange mewling noise she'd never heard him make before, but he seemed unharmed. Well, she'd have to worry about him later, if she could.

"Pogue," she said again. "Cut my arm."

"What? Why?"

"Rolf, keep the crown and ring on. I know what to do," she began. "Pogue, cut my arm."

"You're delirious," Pogue said, panicky. "Should you be delirious so soon?"

"No, I understand," Rolf said slowly. "Yes . . . we probably need . . . Pogue, cut *my* arm, not Cel's."

He held out an arm that was red and blistered like Celie's, shoving his tattered sleeve up to his elbow. Pogue pulled out his dagger, but hesitated.

"Give me the shard, stupid little girl," the Arkower said, edging closer. "Help me gather some griffins, and I'll get you to your precious Sleyne. But first we must restore the balance of our world."

"Our world is dying," Ethan said. "It's plain to see. Just go," he said to Rolf, making an encouraging motion. "Hurry." He leaned closer. "I tried to gather some eggs," he whispered. "They're inside the tomb, safe from fire, I hope."

But the Arkower heard him. "What? Foolish boy," he said, and he backhanded Ethan, knocking him into one of the griffins crowding around them.

"I hate you," Ethan said in a curiously dispassionate voice. "You've doomed our entire world and all because you were jealous of the Hathelockes' pets!"

The Arkower turned to shout at him, but Ethan snatched up a nearly full bucket and upended it over the old man. The Arkower gagged and staggered backward. The griffins surrounding them moved out of his way and he stumbled and fell to the ground.

Pogue grabbed Rolf's arm, apologized, and made the cut. Rolf shook his arm, scattering blood on the wet stones at his feet, and then turned and wiped some on the shard of the Eye that Celie still held, her fingers locked in place.

"Your world doesn't deserve the griffins or the Castle," Celie told them, pleased to find that her voice still worked. She felt very strange, and her vision had gone blurry. She rubbed her face against her shoulder, but her eyes still wouldn't focus properly. "We're taking them home with us."

"Good luck with that, little girl," Bratsch sneered.

"Rolf, do something," Celie said through gritted teeth.

She had had enough of these wizards and their talk. She was frightened that if they didn't return to the Castle soon, she wouldn't be able to see her parents and Bran again. She was frightened, too, for the griffins: Had some of them touched the water? Were they getting the plague? Would they die?

Would she really die?

"I've got this," Rolf said. He coughed. "I've got this . . . we'll just . . ."

"Castle, take us home," Celie said.

"Yes," Rolf said, collecting himself. "Castle, please, take us home. And we want the griffins, the towers, and all."

"Stop it," Bratsch said. He tried to push his way through the crowd of griffins. "Stop that at once, and give me those things. They belong in the Tomb of the Builder!"

"Help us," Celie said to Rufus. She turned her head and gazed blindly at Lord Griffin. "Help us," she said in a louder voice. "Help us."

The griffins closed in, forming a barrier between Celie

and her friends and the wizards. One of the griffins squawked and moved aside to let Ethan through. With a stunned expression, he edged through the golden and brown and cream bodies to stand beside Pogue.

"Help us," Rolf said. "Take us home."

"Take us home," Lilah said.

"Take us home," Pogue echoed.

"Let us be returning to the Castle our home!" Lulath cheered.

Celie pulled the shard of the Eye in close to her chest. She was shaking, her skin burning and her eyes blurred. She was more terrified than she had been when Khelsh had threatened to kill her. All that running and screaming and shouting on the battlements had been almost unreal, and besides, she'd been at the Castle, her home.

Then she realized that this courtyard was also part of the Castle.

"We *are* home," she said under her breath.

Rolf heard her.

"We just want all of our home in Sleyne," he announced.

Instant warmth began to spread over Celie's breastbone, flowing out from the shard of the Eye. It seeped into her skin and though the burns did not subside, they did pain her less. Her vision cleared, and the world stopped moving as though she were on a ship.

"Please, Castle," Pogue muttered. "Just think of it: all the griffins, all your towers, all together and safe! Wouldn't that be nice?" He sounded as though he was talking to a dog.

"Safe in Sleyne," Rolf said.

The stones beneath their feet stirred and shifted. Celie braced herself, pressing her hip against Rufus's side to make sure he wasn't left behind. But nothing happened.

Rolf looked at Celie, desperate. "What do we do?"

Wizard Bratsch cackled. "It won't work! Give me the Eye!"

"The Castle doesn't like you," Celie said. She closed her eyes in despair. The Castle wouldn't risk bringing Bratsch and the Arkower to Sleyne.

"I *built* the Castle," Wizard Bratsch snapped.

"Oh, you did not," Lilah snapped right back. "You just be quiet!" She turned to Lord Griffin. "Get them as far from here as you can," she ordered him. "We'll wait for you!"

Lord Griffin leaped out of the milling crowd of griffins and snatched up a screaming Wizard Bratsch. Another large male griffin followed, picking up the Arkower and flapping away.

The stones began to rumble. Celie half lay across Rufus, fearing that she would faint. She felt an arm around her, and Pogue pulled her up to sit on Rufus's back. He kept his arm around her, bent so that he was holding her arms up, keeping the shard of the Eye pressed to her heart. Rolf was still dripping on the stones, chanting "Safe in Sleyne," with the ring pressed to his brow where the crown rested.

"Here they are coming," Lulath called out.

The two griffins came swooping down and landed in the little space in front of Rolf.

"Now! Take us to Sleyne now!" Rolf shouted.

Celie's world turned upside down. She didn't know where she was, only that Rufus was underneath her and Pogue was beside her. She heard voices, human and griffin. She heard shouting and crashing and squawking and scraping and breaking noises. A furious wind that was both hot and cold tore at her hair and clothes. She thought she heard Pogue saying something to her, but couldn't decipher the words.

And then it all stopped.

They were standing in the courtyard, surrounded by disheveled griffins. To one side was the stable, and across the expanse of yard were two hatching towers.

And beyond the towers was the bulk of the Castle, rising up against a familiar sky.

"You did it," Lilah sobbed. She started to throw her arms around Rolf but stopped just in time. "You did it!"

"I don't feel well," Rolf said, and slumped to the ground.

"You see, Celie, we're home," Pogue said, his voice coming from a long way off.

She tried to nod, but her head felt too heavy. She was gripped with a sudden fear that the griffins would fly out of the Castle and hunt the unicorns, but before she could call out to anyone, she remembered that the unicorns were all gone. She shook her head to clear it, and it felt as though it would roll right off her shoulders.

There were more voices and shouting.

"My darlings," Queen Celina cried, running toward them with her skirts hiked up around her knees. "My darlings!"

"Rolf! Girls!" King Glower was shouting, hard on his wife's heels. "Pogue! Lulath! Praise the skies!"

The queen reached Celie first, and Celie tried to push her mother away so that the poisoned water wouldn't get on her, but the queen didn't care. She swooped down on Celie and covered her with kisses. Then she drew back.

"What's happened to you, my darling?" Her eyes flickered over the others. "Oh, no! And Rolf, too?"

King Glower was hugging and thumping everyone, but when he got to Celie he froze. "Celia-delia," he said in a hushed voice. Then he turned his head and yelled, "*Bran!*"

"I'm here!" Their brother, his official robes flapping, was running across the courtyard. "I'm here—Pogue, thank goodness for your sketches. You were right, my friend, it's all just where you— All right there, Cel?" Bran asked, seeing Celie's face. Then his eyes widened even further. "I see you found the missing bit of the Eye! That's my girl!"

"Just look at her," Queen Celina said in a shrill voice that Celie didn't recognize. "What's wrong? What's happened? And Rolf is affected as well!"

"They are having the poison water, which is the killing of the griffin in the olden times," Lulath said. "Please, Bran, be helping!"

"There's no cure," Ethan muttered. "I'm so sorry. There's no cure."

"Who are you?" King Glower demanded.

"I'm . . . I'm . . . they said I could come," he said, hunching his shoulders like he wanted to sink into the ground.

"He's Ethan," Celie said. Then she coughed. It felt as though there were something stuck in her throat, a chunk of hard bread or something. "He needed to get away from the wizards."

"What wizards?" Queen Celina looked around at her children, her face taut and pale.

She had one arm around Lilah, and another around Lulath, since Celie and Rolf were both warding off anyone who tried to hug them now. There were smudges under her eyes (and their father's), her hair was uncharacteristically wild, and her gown was crumpled, as though she hadn't been sleeping and taking care of her appearance the way she normally would.

"Lulath?" Bran said. He was holding one of Celie's arms up, his hands wrapped in his voluminous sleeves to avoid touching her skin. "Those books of Grathian herbs, are they still in your rooms?"

"Unless they are being taken to a place elsewhere while I am not here," Lulath said. "Yes."

"Good. All right, everyone, let's get them inside the Castle," Bran said loudly. "Lulath, run to your rooms and find those books. We'll be in my rooms."

"What is it? Bran, what's happening?" Queen Celina let go of Lulath, who hurried away with Lorcan still cheeping from inside his tunic. "Bran, tell me!"

"This way, everyone," Bran said, backing toward the Castle doors. "Griffins, too, I suppose."

"Not your rooms," Celie managed to gasp out. "The Heart. The Heart of the Castle."

"Yes, all right," Bran said. "Quickly."

"Bran!" King Glower was anguished.

"They have blackblister," Bran said, walking backward toward the Castle so that they would follow him. "It's a rare disease that crops up in Grath occasionally. I remember it from a book of Lulath's because it's one of the few diseases that both humans and animals can get just from touching each other."

"Fascinating," Queen Celina said, her voice clipped. "But can you cure them?"

"No, Mummy," Celie said. "I'm sorry. There's no cure." She felt her chin wobble. "And Rufus has it, too."

That was the worst blow of all. They'd made it back, they'd healed the Castle, but she and Rolf were dying, and so was Rufus. She'd never get to complete her atlas. Rolf would never be king. Rufus would never be as big as his father.

"Celie," Bran said, stopping in the main hall to look at her. "There is a cure."

Chapter
19

As Bran led the procession of people and griffins into the Heart of the Castle, Wizard Arkwright leaped to his feet. He'd been sitting at one of the benches, studying a book with great unconcern, as though the Castle hadn't just been made whole and the missing prince and princesses returned with a flock of griffins in tow.

Bran left, hurrying to his rooms to get some things he needed. He was already muttering under his breath and moving his hands around in the air, planning some magic.

Celie turned her attention back to the Heart of the Castle. Even feeling as ill as she did, Celie decided that she hated Arkwright, sitting there gaping at them. Also, even with her blurred vision, she could see that he was about to lie. Really, the man was a terrible actor, and it was impressive that he had managed to conceal his origins and the history of the Castle for so long.

"Get back," Arkwright said in a voice thick with terror. He looked over Celie's head to the king and queen. "It's the plague. The plague that killed my people and our griffins years ago! It's highly contagious, and I'm afraid there is no cure." He made a warding gesture at Rolf, who was walking toward him, supported by Pogue. "Please, Your Highness, come no closer. You endanger us all!"

"Your people never had griffins," Rolf said coldly. "That was just the first of your many lies."

Arkwright opened his mouth, then closed it again. His expression took on a mixture of curiosity and cunning that made him look even more unpleasant than usual.

"Here is being the books," Lulath said, running into the room.

"If Bran says that there's a cure, and that this happens in Grath, too, I believe him," Lilah said.

"It is true what our Bran the Wizard is saying, it is happening in the Grath, from time and again," Lulath asserted, seeing the queen's panicked look. "There is being a cure, O Our Majesty.

"And I am now of the thought that it is being brought from the Arkish lands, yes," Lulath continued. "From those who are living on the shore with themselves kept to themselves." He shook his head. "I am only now seeing, they must be having been the griffin riders who are living, which griffins did follow these unicorns to the sea."

Celie stuck that in the back of her brain. She would have

to ask Lulath more questions about it, when she wasn't dying.

"Are they the people who don't speak Grathian, or any other language anyone knows?" Lilah asked. Celie vaguely remembered Lulath telling them about these people weeks ago, during their own Grathian lessons.

"Indeed," Lulath said. "Perhaps now it is our Ethan who could be telling us where these are the people of! The Glorious Arkower? Hathelocke? After we are curing our friends, of course," he added.

"What?" Wizard Arkwright spun around to glare at Lulath. "You don't know what you're talking about! Arkish people in Grath! Madness! And there is no cure! And no way of fixing the Eye!"

"So *you* hope," Lilah said coldly. "Father, I want him locked up! His uncle tried to kill us, and he's just as horrible!"

"I agree," Rolf said woozily. "Guards!" His shout frightened the maids hovering in the doorway. "Guards!"

Several guards came running. They had clearly been waiting, hoping to be needed so that they could find out what was happening. One of them saluted Rolf. The others remembered the king and hastily put their hands to their helmets.

"Lock this man up," Rolf said, pointing to Arkwright with a blistered, shaking finger. "He's a traitor and has aided in the murders of countless men and griffins."

"How dare you—" Arkwright began as the guards seized his arms.

But the king had also signaled to the guards, who dragged the protesting wizard away. "Insufferable man," King Glower said. "I'm glad to hear he's a traitor. Now I can justify my dislike of him."

"Is there really a cure?" Queen Celina was looking anxiously at Celie and Rolf, but Celie noticed that she had blisters on her hands from touching them. She saw Celie looking and hid her hands in her sleeves.

"For every very blessed ill there is being a cure," Lulath said complacently.

"We have to cure the Castle first," Celie said. She let go of Rufus's harness and took a few tottering steps. Her ears felt full of cotton wool, and she didn't think anyone heard her, so she said it again, louder.

"We have to cure the Castle first."

"Agreed," Rolf said. "Put me down, Pogue."

Pogue, who had half carried Rolf inside, reluctantly took his arm from Rolf's shoulders. Rolf stood unsteadily in front of their father. Then he took the crown off his head and held it out to King Glower. The king was bareheaded: he generally wore his crown only during formal occasions.

"The crown of the Builder of the Castle," Rolf said. And, when their father made no move to touch it, "Take it. It's yours now."

King Glower started to protest, but he saw Rolf's face

and Celie's, Lilah's and Pogue's and Lulath's. He hesitated, brows knit.

"Daddy," Celie said. "Didn't you hear? It's the crown, the real crown. The Builder of the Castle's crown."

The king paused a moment more, then solemnly took the crown and placed it on his own head.

"And now the other ring of the Builder," Rolf said, and offered up the ring.

King Glower took it without protest and put it on his left hand. On his right was the griffin ring that every King Glower had worn. King Glower looked down at his hands, then reached up to feel the crown. The stones of the Castle stirred and then settled, as though a sigh had run through the Castle, and through those watching. Rolf nodded.

The griffins around them suddenly stiffened. They left off sniffing at the tapestries and furnishings, and turned to face King Glower. The largest of them, Rufus's father, gave a stiff little bow and voiced a piercing cry. When the sound of the griffin's cry died away, King Glower took a few steps forward and then looked anxiously at Celie.

"Should I bow?" he said in a hoarse whisper.

"I don't know," Celie answered, and Rolf shrugged.

The king inclined his head, and that seemed to be the right thing to do. Lord Griffin bowed again, and then he and his companions dispersed themselves about the room, lying down in corners and on the cold hearth.

"I wonder if he'd let us put that collar on him," Pogue mused.

"You're welcome to try," Rolf said.

"Maybe later," Pogue said.

"Now for the missing piece of the Eye," Celie announced. She turned. It felt as though she was going to keep turning and she nearly fell.

"Celie!" Queen Celina cried.

"Bran!" the king roared. "Where are you?"

"I've got you," Pogue said, scooping her up.

"The plague," Celie said weakly, and tried to squirm out of his arms.

"For every blessed thing there is being a cure," Pogue reminded her, quoting Lulath with a half smile. "I've already touched Rolf, anyway."

Celie laughed, then coughed. Pogue carried her through the collection of tapestries, maps, cushions, and other bric-a-brac bearing images of griffins that had been neatly arranged on the long tables. At the far end, above the fireplace, the Eye had been placed in its niche, making the missing part all the more obvious. Pogue shifted Celie in his arms so that she was sitting up, and Celie very carefully matched up the piece of dull and dirty stone with its clean and shining other half.

The Castle shivered.

After a long pause, as though even the Castle was holding its breath, the two parts of the Eye melted together. The dirty side was made clean and new, and every stone of the Castle seemed to sit up, and sparkled, just briefly, before settling back into place.

The silence was broken by Lulath letting out a cheer.

"O huzzah! Is not it the wonder?" he cried.

Celie burst out laughing, helpless.

"Is it done? Is it over?" Lilah demanded. "That seemed too easy."

"I'd say yes," King Glower said. "It's over, I mean, not that it was too easy. Nothing so far has been easy.

"Let's get Celie and Rolf upstairs," he added.

"Right here is just fine," Rolf said.

Now that her hands were empty, Celie realized how itchy her blisters were. Her eyes were getting even blurrier, and her head felt foggy. She rested her head on Pogue's shoulder.

"How did those riders make it to Sleyne before, without knowing they were sick?" Rolf asked as Pogue put Celie down beside him on a bench. The queen came to fuss over them, pushing back Celie's hair and looking into both their eyes. She turned her head and called an order to the maids, but Celie didn't catch what her mother had asked for. Her hearing seemed to be going in and out. Rufus curled up at her feet and put his head on her lap. She put trembling hands on his head.

"They probably didn't get a bucket of poisonous water dumped on their heads," Pogue said drily.

"I need to know what's happened, but I'm almost too terrified to ask," Queen Celina said. "And where on earth is Bran?"

"Coming, coming," Bran called, running into the room with an armload of books and bottles.

Celie slumped against Rolf and closed her eyes.

"Bran, what do you need?" Pogue said.

Bran began issuing instructions to Pogue and their mother, who Celie had almost forgotten had magical skill. She let herself drift, holding a prayer in her heart that Bran could cure them, and quickly. She could feel Rufus's head shivering under her hands.

"Cel," Rolf said, interrupting her as she started to fall asleep. "Hey Cel? What should we do after we get better?"

Celie couldn't answer him. She couldn't understand how he was still talking. It took all her strength just to sit.

"Your Highness," Ethan said humbly to Rolf. "Can we not get the other eggs?"

"Oh, I'd nearly forgotten them," Rolf said. "Yes, we shall do that!"

"What eggs?" King Glower said. "Who are you again?"

"Your Majesty," Ethan said, and his voice faded in and out as though he were bowing. "I was an assistant to the Arkower, the last Arkish wizard. I helped him . . . attempt to . . . train griffins. I have gathered three eggs and hidden them in the Tomb of the Builder, so that we could collect them later."

"Griffin eggs?" King Glower sounded amazed. "You found *three* griffin eggs? And three actual griffins will hatch from them?"

"To add to the ones you've brought with you?" Queen Celina said with amusement. "Where will we put them all?"

"We now have two griffin stables," King Glower said. "Wait . . . how did I know that?"

"It's the crown," Rolf said. "I wore it for a few minutes, and I could *feel* the Castle."

Celie felt a flutter of jealousy but was too sick to indulge it.

"You're the griffin trainer," Lilah whispered to her, sitting down at her side. "And don't you forget it. I need your help with Juliet, as soon as you feel better."

"Thank you," Celie whispered back, and felt tears sting her blurry eyes.

They sat in silence, and Celie started to drift off again.

"All right, Cel, here we go," Bran said a moment later. "Drink this."

She tried to open her eyes, and realized that she couldn't. Lilah and Pogue were holding her up, and she could hear Queen Celina saying something to Rolf, but Rolf wasn't answering.

A cold metal cup touched her lower lip and she managed to open her mouth enough for Bran to tilt some of the potion down her throat. She heard Lulath talking expansively about Lorcan to her father. Heard her mother urging Rolf to drink. She had to make the muscles of her throat work by sheer force of will.

The cup was taken away and Lilah pulled her over so

that she was resting against her sister's shoulder. Rufus stirred in her lap, and she felt something wet drip onto her foot.

"Will you just *drink*, you little monster," Bran said in exasperation.

"And all who are touching the Celie and the Rolf will be drinking this the last," Lulath said. "Our lovely queen, I am seeing your beautiful poor hands!"

"Do you feel better yet?" Lilah whispered.

Celie tried to blink, but her eyes felt gummy. Bran took hold of her chin and rubbed something that felt and smelled like mud on her eyelids, then washed it away with a wet cloth. When he was done, she opened her eyes and her vision started to clear.

"Daddy?"

"What is it, Celia-delia?" King Glower almost tripped over Rufus trying to get to her.

"I'm starving," she said, marveling at the sudden feeling of hunger replacing the aches and pains of the plague. "Can you ask the Castle to bring me a custard from the kitchens?"

"Ask it yourself," the king said fondly. "You're still its favorite."

Chapter
20

$\mathcal{S}$ir Pogue, would you hand me that blanket?" Rolf called.

"Please stop calling me that," Pogue begged.

"But you are being now Sir Pogue!" Lulath cried. "What honor! What excitement!"

Celie grabbed one of the folded blankets and threw it at Rolf. It unfolded in the air and landed with a soft whump on the egg he was wrapping. Rolf grinned at her and shook out the blanket, tucking it carefully around the egg.

"Can we hurry, please?" Lilah said. She looked around nervously. "I really hate this place."

Celie had to agree. The Glorious Arkower—Hatheland— whatever you wanted to call it, was no place that anyone would want to be. Not anymore.

The fire had died out, though smoke still choked the air. Most of the trees were gone, and the blackened waste extended all the way to the foot of the Arkower's mountain. Where the Castle ruins had been was just a black plain, with no sign that anything had ever been there. Away in the distance, toward the city where Ethan had been born, the trees started up again, screening the city from their view. Rolf had asked Ethan if he wanted to go back there, or even find a way to send a message, but Ethan had declined.

"To whom would I send a message?" Ethan had asked. "I have no one, and nowhere to go."

"You have the Castle," King Glower had said firmly. "This is your home now."

He had made Ethan a ward of the court, which the queen explained to the stunned young man meant that he could live in the Castle and take lessons with Master Humphries like Celie and Rolf. That was just after Pogue had been knighted for his "services to the Castle and the Glower family," which Rolf had cheerfully translated as "saving everyone's lives repeatedly even after being hit on the head."

Once Celie and Rolf and Rufus had recovered from the plague—which took four days of treatments, while they suffered from fever, chills, and a ravenous appetite that Rolf swore was really just the effect of the lack of decent food in Hatheland—and the queen and Pogue had been treated for mild cases of it, they had wanted to return immediately for the eggs. But King Glower had insisted that they wait. They had told their story to the king and queen and

Bran, and then to the rest of the court. They had bathed and changed and eaten and slept, and been commended for their valor separately and in a group.

Then, after a week, the king said that they had waited long enough. The wizards would have let their guard down, the fire would not still be burning. Celie by then was nearly wild with nerves, and so were the others. They didn't want any of the eggs to hatch alone inside the tomb. They wanted them to hatch safely inside one of the new hatching towers, where the grown griffins could watch over them.

"And a few of us could maybe, just maybe, have a chance of bonding with them," Rolf had put in.

It had taken a little time to convince the king and queen that they did not need to take the entire army with them, and to negotiate down to just Bran, four soldiers, and King Glower and Queen Celina. Then there had been the problem of how to get there. They could tell the Castle to send them—or so they thought—but how would they get back?

"We'll have to take a piece of the Castle with us," Celie had pointed out. "It's probably easiest if it's a bit that already sticks out, but without a lot of stairs to climb."

That ruled out any of the towers, and it was Rolf who pointed out that the piece of the Castle that jutted out the farthest was in fact the griffin stable where Celie had found the piece of the Eye. So they had all gathered there and huddled around the king, who clenched his fists and screwed his eyes shut, muttering under his breath to the Castle.

The twist in the back of Celie's head came, there was a rumble, and the smell of smoke wafted through the open door. Turning, they saw that the door no longer opened onto the rear courtyard, but onto a barren, burned plain.

And now here they were at the Tomb of the Builder, carefully loading the eggs onto canvas stretchers, wrapping them in blankets, and getting ready to take them back to Sleyne. They had, of course, taken their parents on a hushed tour of the tomb first, while the soldiers waited outside and fidgeted, grabbing their sword hilts every time the wind gusted.

Rolf wrapped the last egg and signaled to Pogue. Together they lifted a stretcher with an egg on it and carefully maneuvered out of the tomb. Lulath and Bran took up another, and Ethan and King Glower himself got the third. Once they were all outside the tomb, those not carrying eggs surrounded the stretchers, looking anxiously for any sign of the wizards.

But there was no sign of them. There was no sign of anything alive.

They couldn't even find Wizard Bratsch's hut. There were so many identical charred lumps that had been boulders or trees that it had taken them much longer than they'd thought to locate the tomb, let alone find the small, makeshift house.

Lord and Lady Griffin had come with them, Lord Griffin proudly wearing the gold collar that had belonged to the Builder's griffin, but they had refused to let Rufus join the party and Celie had agreed with them. Lorcan and Juliet were likewise deemed too young, and so they had stayed with Rufus in his exercise tower, where he was showing them how to destroy a leather ball. Once they reached the Glorious Arkower, the adult griffins would not leave the stable anyway, and were standing just inside the door when Celie and the others got back with the eggs.

Lord Griffin inspected the eggs thoroughly, yanking aside the blanket wrappings with his beak and sniffing and eyeing each one in turn. Once he was satisfied, they all shuffled inside. King Glower was just getting ready to ask the Castle to take them home when a pair of wild griffins arrived.

Lord Griffin went out to them at once, while Lady Griffin and the rest of them hovered in the doorway. The wild griffins and Lord Griffin all clacked and squawked and rustled their wings. Then the wild griffins turned and flew away.

"Come back! Come with us," Celie called, but they just kept going. Lord Griffin gently butted her back into the stable. "They should come with us," she said, pointing to the floor.

But the king of the griffins squawked what was undoubtedly a no. He looked expectantly at King Glower and carked, and the king shrugged at Celie and began to exhort the Castle to take them home.

A twist and a whoosh and they were back in Sleyne.

Rolf immediately commandeered the soldiers with them to help take the largest of the eggs (which he was making no secret of wanting to bond with) up to one of the hatching towers. Bran and the king saw to the other two, and griffins came flooding out of the other stable to look at the eggs and make excited sounds. It all made Celie feel rather muzzy and tired, so she retreated to her rooms to see Rufus.

He had taken all the treats and toys and put them in one corner of the play tower, which he was now defending. Celie promptly pulled him away and let Juliet and Lorcan get some of the treats, threatening Rufus with his toy enemy, Flat Squirrel, when he wouldn't share.

Lilah soon joined them, and Juliet careened into her "mother's" lap with great delight. They played with the griffins for a little while, and then Lilah coughed and looked at Celie thoughtfully.

"You know, Celie," Lilah said. "I don't want to sound greedy . . ."

"You don't want to sound greedy, but . . . ?" Celie raised her eyebrows.

"I already have Juliet, and I love her so much, don't get me wrong."

"But . . . ?" Celie asked again.

"But don't you think it would be exciting to go on another adventure?" Lilah smiled winningly at Celie.

"An adventure where?" Celie looked at her sister sideways. Lilah actually proposing an adventure, as opposed to suggesting they go shopping for fun? What was this really about?

"I mean, I don't want to leave anytime soon," Lilah went on. "We've only just gotten home, and there are so many new things in the Castle to explore. But we both speak Grathian, and it seems like such a shame to waste our talent." She smiled a little secret smile. "And I'm sure Lulath's family would welcome us with open arms."

"You want to go to Grath?" That made much more sense: Grath was famous for its lace and silk. Also, since their return Lilah and Lulath had twice been caught kissing in corners. Celie relaxed. A trip to Grath sounded rather pleasant.

"Well," Lilah said. "I mean to say that we'd go to Grath first. I'd be a fool not to do a little shopping . . . and meet Lulath's family. Besides, you're growing like a weed; you could use a new, more grown-up wardrobe. But what I was really thinking about was that Grath is the place where the unicorns fled. And then, you know, they were taken onto ships that sailed away. And I've always loved unicorns." She raised her eyebrows at Celie.

Celie's heart began to pound. "That's very true, you do love unicorns. And I have always wanted to see the sea."

Acknowledgments

Writing a book never gets easier, much to my great surprise, which is why I consider myself so lucky to have so many wonderful people supporting me!

First of all, this book had three fabulous editors who worked hard to make it really shine. So big hugs and thanks to Michelle Nagler, Caroline Abbey, and Mary Kate Castellani! You are all amazing, and I am so lucky to have been able to work with you! And thanks to all the wonderful Bloomsbury folks: Cindy Loh, Bridget Hartzler, Beth Eller, Brett Wright, Lizzy Mason, Cristina Gilbert, Emily Ritter, Erica Barmash, Hali Baumstein . . . I adore you all! Thanks to former Bloomsbury peep Katy Hershberger, for setting up (and coming along on) my first ever book tour, which was such brilliant fun!

Thanks, so much thanks, to my dear agent and friend, Amy Jameson, for being so many things I'm not, like patient and organized. And thanks for the encouragement, and the delicious conversations over delicious lunches!

There is no way to properly thank my family, who make it possible for me to be a writer. How do you say thank you for years of love and support and awesomeness? It's just too hard, so just know that I love you all!

And a great big hug and a thank-you to all the readers who have shown so much love for Celie and her Castle! You're all fabulous!

EXCLUSIVE!

Read on for a special bonus story,
"An Afternoon at the Castle"

Every autumn, Celie and her siblings play
a special game on the Castle grounds:
Capture the Crown! Can Celie outsmart
her brothers *and* the castle to win the day?

It's the day! Today's the day!" Someone pounced on Celie and ripped the blankets away from her face. "Why are you sleeping? Today's the day!"

Celie threw off the rest of her blankets, causing the little cousin who had attacked her to tumble backward onto the foot of Celie's wide bed. Celie hadn't actually been asleep . . . in fact, she was fully dressed and had been lying carefully beneath the blankets so that her mother wouldn't peep in and scold her for getting up too early.

It was the first day of the Harvest Festival, and that meant the Game.

Every year on the first day of the Festival, after the crops had all been brought in from the fields, the Castle created a game for the children as part of the festivities. A hedge maze would grow—overnight!—in the sheep meadow just outside the Castle walls, but the entrance to

the maze could be anywhere inside the Castle. At the center of the maze was a laurel crown of gold that the winner
got to wear at the Harvest Feast.

The Castle never played favorites when it came to the
Game, and so Celie didn't have any advantage over her
siblings or cousins. Rolf had won the crown for the past
three years, and Bran, before he left for the College of
Wizardry, had held the record with five straight wins.

Celie had never won, but she was determined to this
year. Now that Bran was the Royal Wizard, she wasn't
sure that he would be participating. She normally didn't
like it when Bran claimed to be too grown up to have fun,
but in this case she hoped he would. It was becoming
embarrassing that she hadn't won, since she was widely
known to be the only person who had never gotten lost in
the Castle, and this year she was armed with her com-
pleted maps.

"Yes," she told her cousin, six-year-old Sera. "It's today."

"You're already dressed!" Sera goggled at her. "That's
cheating!"

"It is not cheating," Celie said with as much dignity as
she could muster. "We all start at the same time. But if
you don't want to miss the start, you'll have to hurry."

Celie followed her cousin out the door and ran for the
Heart of the Castle, formerly the holiday feasting hall,
where food was laid out for breakfast. She stuffed a sweet
roll in her mouth and put two more in a napkin, which
went into her satchel. She also put a handful of berries

into another napkin, and a boiled egg. The Game could go all day long, and she wasn't about to get distracted by hunger.

"Sit down and eat something like a young lady," Lilah said from the end of the table.

She was calmly buttering a piece of toast. Her hair and gown were impeccable, as always, and Celie was glad that yet another of her siblings was too old for the Game. Lilah, for all her fussing about her appearance, could be extremely wily.

Across from her, Prince Lulath of Grath was feeding bits of sausage to his dogs, who were all standing on their hind legs to get closer to the treat. Lulath, who didn't eat meat, also had a plate heaped with fruit and rolls. He grinned at Celie.

"What the excitement today, is it not being? A game!"

"*The* Game," Celie corrected him. "This is the only game the Castle plays."

"Such the excitement!" Lulath said again. "I am only doing the watching, from the very Spyglass Tower! My girls, and my Lorcan, will be so enjoying the spectacular!"

Lorcan was Lulath's half-grown griffin, who was probably in the griffin tower with Celie's Rufus and Lilah's Juliet, tearing into their own breakfast. Celie would normally hurry to feed Rufus herself . . . but just this once, on the day of the Game, Celie thought her darling Rufus could get by without her.

"I would not be thinking to try for myself to take part!"

Lulath said, disarranging his elaborately brushed and waved hair with an emphatic shake of his head.

"Oh, come now, Lulath," Rolf said, strolling into the room and taking up a plate. "I'm sure you'd be brilliant! You've been all over the Castle and the grounds; you might as well join us."

"Yes, why don't you team up with Rolf?" Bran said, coming into the dining hall as well.

He started filling a satchel with food, and Celie's heart sank. Bran *was* going to going to play the Game! Now her chances were even worse. She took some more food and decided to go out and wait in the throne room for the start. As she left the hall, she heard Rolf frantically trying to get out of helping Lulath without mortally offending the good-natured Grathian prince.

"Your dogs would absolutely hate it," Rolf said as Celie closed the doors behind her. "And what about Lorcan?"

Crossing the entrance hall, she ran into her aunt Mellie and Sera, who was now dressed. Aunt Mellie gave her a big smile.

"Excited for the Game, Celie?"

"Oh, yes," Celie said. She was walking quickly, trying to not obviously leave them behind, but just look very busy.

"I have my money on Celie this year," Uncle Penrod said, catching up to them. "After your adventures fighting off that Vhervhish chappie and healing the Castle itself, I think the Castle might be extra grateful to you," he said with a meaningful wink.

Celie resented the idea that the Castle might help her, but she knew that Uncle Penrod meant well, and just smiled and shrugged.

"I've just had an idea, my dears," her uncle continued, herding them through the open doors into the throne room, which was filling up with bright-eyed children and young people eager to start the Game. Uncle Penrod beamed from his daughter Sera to Celie, and then waggled his eyebrows at Aunt Mellie. "Why not have clever Celie help Sera? Last year she didn't even find the entrance to the maze! Spent the whole day wandering the servants' quarters," he reminded Celie.

Celie nodded, not sure what to say. She dearly loved Sera, but Sera couldn't run as fast as she could, or climb out on the roofs . . . in fact, if Aunt Mellie or Uncle Penrod saw Celie trying to help Sera out a tower window they would probably panic and call a halt to the whole Game.

Looking around the throne room for help, Celie caught her mother's eye. Queen Celina raised one eyebrow and started toward her, but Aunt Mellie came to the rescue first. She pointed to the windows, where the other small cousins were gathering, and then put a hand on her husband's arm.

"Dear, that's a lovely idea, but it's the *Game*," she said patiently. She smiled at Celie. "That Castle doesn't help anyone, and no one works in teams. There is one crown and one winner." Aunt Mellie, Celie's mother's sister, had grown up in the Castle, and as the younger daughter of the Royal Wizard, she knew how things worked. "My money's on Celie as well, but not if she has to drag one of our children with her!" She raised one finger to forestall her husband's objection. "And as a mother, I have no desire to see my daughter climbing the roofs of the Castle!"

"Who's going to be climbing on the roofs?" Celie's mother joined them, twining an arm around her sister's waist.

"Celie, most likely," Aunt Mellie said.

"Oh, now, I don't think Celie would resort to such improper and dangerous behavior," Uncle Penrod said.

"She undoubtedly will," Queen Celina said. "And I gave up trying to stop her years ago." She reached out her free hand and pushed Celie's hair off her shoulders. "Count your blessings that Sera hasn't shown an interest in the roofs yet."

"Who's going up on the roof? Celie?" Rolf came in with Lilah and Lulath. "Nah! The Castle's never put anything up there. Too far from the maze!" He was rubbing his hands together eagerly.

"You're heading to the roofs, Cel?" Bran was the last one in the throne room, and he studied Celie keenly. "That would certainly be something new and different. And if the Castle were going to play favorites—"

"The Castle won't play favorites," Celie said, stung. She wanted to win, but she'd do it fair and square.

"All right, is everyone ready?" Celie's father, King

Glower, went to stand in front of his throne. He rubbed his hands together in a gesture much like Rolf's.

Celie, her siblings, her cousins, and the young people from the village all crowded closer to the dais. Pogue Parry noticed that Celie was standing on tiptoe, and nudged his sisters to move out of the way so that Celie could move closer to the foot of the dais. She gave him a quick, grateful smile, and he winked in return. Pogue had nearly gotten the crown the past two years, and he would definitely be one to beat.

"Welcome to the Harvest Festival and the Game," King Glower said. "I see many young faces who were not old enough last year, and many faces that I thought would be too old this year." He tilted his head toward Bran, and everyone laughed. Bran shrugged.

"It's my first year as Royal Wizard," Bran called out. "I need the break."

"You all know the rules . . . which are that there really are none. The Castle has provided a maze, with a crown at its center, and the way through the maze and *into* the maze are known only to the Castle. Be careful, be kind, and if you need help, all you need to do is turn in a circle three times and say, "Castle, send help." The Castle will lead an adult to you."

He glanced at the windows, through which the autumn sun was just beginning to shine.

"It's time! Go!"

Everyone turned and streamed out of the throne room.

Celie immediately broke away from the group and ran for the stairs to the Spyglass Tower. Lulath talking about watching the Game from there had given her an idea. From the Spyglass Tower, with its magical spyglasses, she'd be able to see the maze. And if she could see the maze, she might be able to see the tunnel that led into it.

She could hear people mounting the stairs behind her but wasn't sure if it was Lulath and Lilah (who was never far from Lulath these days), or some of her cousins hoping for help. She sped up, and was hot and sweaty by the time she reached the top of the tower.

The maze in the sheep meadow was on the east side of the Castle, and so was the Spyglass Tower. She ran to the window and leaned out, peering over the side to catch a view of the maze.

It was magnificent.

High green hedges twisted and swirled across the meadow. It made a pattern that looked almost familiar, and Celie wondered if it made a picture when seen from directly above or from another side. In the very center was a circular chamber—she could see that much, but even from the tower she couldn't see the crown inside it.

"She's up here," she heard someone call from the stairs.

Celie looked around, but the secret passage out of the Spyglass Tower was gone, which meant there was only one way out. Gritting her teeth, she headed for the stairs, not happy about having to push past everyone coming up.

Her scalp prickled, and she gave a small cheer, looking

around eagerly. It seemed that the Castle was going to help her after all!

There was a small chute next to the stairs now, and she didn't hesitate. She gathered her skirts around her knees and hopped into it.

She shot down the chute at a terrifying speed and landed on a pile of cushions in the corridor just outside her own bedroom. She leaped up and started down the corridor to the main hall. There were several adults milling around there, including her parents. Her father gave her a wave, then shrugged when she drew a question mark in the air with one finger.

Good, the entrance hadn't been found yet. She turned around and ran back down the corridor. As she ran, she thought back over the list of entrances from the past ten years. She'd written them all down last night, then committed the list to memory and burned the paper. It had been in the kitchens last year, and before that, the laundry. But before that it had been a slide that ran from one of the windows of the north tower all the way over the outer wall and down into the maze. It had also been in the throne room (there was no sign of it there today, obviously), in the stables, and in the winter dining hall.

Celie was on her way up the stairs, thinking to look in the schoolroom, when she froze. It had been in the schoolroom before, though not for many years. It had been in the dining halls, the stables . . . If it was somewhere different every year, and it had already been in all those places . . .

There was only one place, or rather, one kind of place, it hadn't been in at least a decade.

The bedchambers.

No one had found the entrance to the maze in a bedchamber for as far back as anyone could remember. But which bedchamber would it be? Now that the Castle was whole there were bedchambers galore, filled to bursting with her aunts, uncles, and cousins who were visiting for the Harvest Festival. There were also the rooms for her family and the servants who lived in the Castle, like Ma'am Housekeeper and Cook.

"That's a lot of rooms," Celie said in despair.

But she still had a good feeling about it. She headed back down the stairs and stopped outside the first bedchamber on the left. Hmm. Lilah's? Unlikely, but that was the point, so it was definitely worth a try. Celie tossed the door open with a dramatic flourish.

Nothing.

Of course, Lilah spent a great deal of time in her room every morning, making herself perfect, so it probably hadn't been the best choice. The Castle wouldn't have had time to make any changes. But what about the servants? Celie wondered. They were up before everyone else, and rarely went back to their rooms during the day, which would make it easier for the Castle to make changes in their rooms.

Outside of Bran's bedchamber, however, she froze again.

The Castle didn't play favorites (barring the slide it had just created for Celie), but it did like to put the entrance in the least likely place. And the least likely bedchamber would be either Bran's or Rolf's, as the most recent champions, or hers, as the Castle's favorite (or so everyone said).

Celie grabbed the latch on Bran's door and threw it open. This was actually Bran's wizard's workroom, so she ran through to peek inside his bedchamber. Both were terribly messy, since he didn't let the maids in to clean, but there was no entrance unless it was under the bed, which seemed far too odd, even for the Castle.

Celie continued on to her room. She wasn't even looking as she threw open the door, already planning to run across the front hall to Rolf's bedchamber, but something caught her eye.

The large narrow windows of her bedchamber were gone.

In their place was a single arched doorway with no door, and through it an endless corridor of dark green. A brisk autumn breeze blew through the curtains of her bed and tapped gently at her face. Celie stifled a little scream of excitement. She leaped through the door to her bedchamber and closed it behind her. She thought for a moment about locking it, but that wasn't very sporting, so she left it and ran across the room to the doorway.

Celie paused on the threshold. Beyond it the sun was shining, and the green hedge curved away to the left, leading off the courtyard (she assumed—she couldn't actually see over it) and into the sheep meadow. Celie straightened her satchel, took a deep breath, and stepped into the maze.

There were no twists or turns yet, just the curve of dry autumn hedge. Celie ran along it, her feet making no noise on the turf floor of the maze, and her ears pricked as she listened for sounds of pursuit. She didn't hear anything yet, which was a good sign. She came to the first turning and chose right, toward the center of the maze.

Another twist and it proved to be a dead end. Celie backtracked, and at the entrance to that path, she reached into her satchel and pulled out a small pebble. She'd spent yesterday afternoon surreptitiously gathering some distinctive white stones, and now she placed the pebble to one side of the path entrance, almost under the hedge.

The dead end marked, she went on to the left to the next turning, and went right again, trying to get to the center. Then right again: another dead end, quickly marked. The next path swooped around near the Castle again, and Celie clearly heard Rolf's voice, and the excited squeaking of some young cousins. It sounded like they'd found the entrance to the maze, and she broke into a run.

Celie didn't get far, though, before a stitch in her side made her stop. That and she almost went right by a turning. She looked down each branch and decided to continue to the right. This one looped back toward the Castle again, but she still had a sense that she was moving closer to the center of the maze.

Stopping to think at the next branching, she heard a sound very close. She looked around, startled. It couldn't be! It sounded like Lulath's dogs yapping, but even if he had changed his mind about playing, he wouldn't have brought his girls, would he?

There was a rustling in the hedge near Celie's feet. Celie backed slowly away.

Then a small caramel-and-white figure popped out of the thick hedge and ran at her, barking and wagging its tail.

"JouJou!" Celie stared in astonishment. "You shouldn't be here!"

"Our Celie?" Lulath's voice carried clearly over the hedge. "Are you being nearby to me?"

"Lulath," Celie called. "I'm here, I've got JouJou . . ." She fought down her frustration. You weren't supposed to use dogs to track other players! Or distract them! She had to remind herself that good-natured Lulath probably wasn't trying to do either. JouJou was almost as fond of Celie as Rufus was, and often followed her around.

"I am being that sorry, our Celie," Lulath called. "I am not thinking to play this game, but my girls, they are sniffing down the door and going before into the maze, and I am going only to find them! I have not a wish for the crown!"

"I've got JouJou safe and sound," she called back, trying not to lose her patience. She tried futilely to stuff the little dog back through the hole in the hedge without hurting her, but JouJou was having none of it. "I'll just . . . carry on . . . with her," Celie said finally. She was starting to sweat, and other voices were growing louder and closer.

"It is being well, our Celie," Lulath shouted back. "I may be going back if I am not lost. If I am having lost my way, I may be having to go on to finish this Game. Put my bad girl down: JouJou is being safe enough."

"All right," Celie called in reply.

She set the little dog down on the turf and started trotting the way she'd been going before the interruption. JouJou stayed on her heels, panting happily. At the next branching Celie turned left, and ran straight into Bran.

She stared at him in horror before blurting out, "Bran! How did you get ahead of me?" She'd thought she had at least half an hour's head start, but Bran and even Lulath had caught up to her.

"There's more than one path, Cel, it's a maze," Bran pointed out.

Celie just huffed impatiently and went past him, not willing to lose more time by stopping.

"Cel!" Bran shouted after her.

"What?" She didn't look back.

"Dead end!"

She looked down the path she'd started on. It looked like a perfectly good path to her. There were no turnings as far as she could see, but it curved sharply in the direction of the center.

"I promise, Cel, no tricks," Bran said. "It's a dead end."

Celie wasted a precious moment studying her brother, but she knew he wouldn't trick her. She muttered thanks and pushed past him to go the other way. He followed, because there was no other way to go but back. At the next turning they ran into Rolf.

"Dead end," he said, jerking his thumb over his shoulder at the way he'd come.

"The same," Bran said, pointing back the way he and Celie had come. "Shall we?"

They all three turned and went down the only remaining untried turning, with JouJou at their heels. Celie's stomach was churning. How was she going to get rid of her brothers so that she could get to the center of the maze and win? They were far into the maze now, and there would be only one way into the center. If they just had to run for it, Rolf was the fastest runner in their family.

They took another turning together, and another, because they seemed like the best way. Rolf gave them a questioning look at each junction, and Celie and Bran shrugged and followed. There was no point in going what was clearly the wrong way just to get away from the others.

Celie's heart was sinking lower and lower when JouJou stopped and started barking and digging at the base of one of the hedges. Celie whistled at her and kept on walking with her brothers, but JouJou squealed and backed away like something had hurt her. With a sigh, Celie went back to the little dog.

"Coming, Cel?" Bran and Rolf were standing at the mouth of another path that looked like it led straight to the center.

Celie grimaced and took a step toward them. JouJou squealed again, and Celie waved her brothers on with a sigh. She stooped down and picked up the little dog, her exasperation turning to concern when she saw that there were prickles from the hedge in the dog's tiny black nose.

"Oh, poor baby!"

Celie crouched down and balanced the dog on her knees, carefully tweezing the prickles out with her fingernails. She ignored the sick feeling in her stomach that told her she'd just lost the crown yet again. There was no way she could keep walking and let JouJou suffer.

"How did this happen? I didn't think the hedge was that prickly," Celie said, more to soothe the dog with her voice than anything else.

When she was done, she stood up and tucked the dog under her arm like a parcel and looked at the hedge where JouJou had gotten the prickles. It was a different type of hedge from the rest of the maze, and it looked . . . odd. It was a faintly darker shade of green, as well as having prickles, and there seemed to be only one narrow patch of it.

Celie shrugged, and turned to continue on. But in turning her head, she saw that it was shaped like a doorway. She reached out a hand and touched the place where it met the rest of the hedge.

"Ouch!"

The prickles stabbed at her hand.

"Why is that even there?" Celie grumbled, and turned away again.

But again, as she turned her head, the look of the hedge stopped her. It really did look like a door. And now she saw that the center of it was shimmering faintly. She put out a hand, gently, and barely touched one of the leaves in the middle.

It didn't prick her; it tingled.

JouJou barked, and her rear end wiggled. Celie shifted the dog to a more comfortable hold and took a deep breath.

"All right," she said. "Let's just see, shall we?"

She positioned herself directly in front of the "doorway," looking around first to make sure that no one was watching. Not only did she not want to give away a secret passage, if she was lucky enough to find one, but also, if it wasn't a door and she just got a faceful of hedge, she didn't want anyone to see.

It tingled as she passed through the hedge door. On the other side, she blinked some sparkles out of her eyes, and stared in wonder.

Celie found herself in a little round hedge room with no other entrances. In the center was a waist-high pillar of stone, and on the pillar was a crown.

The crown. The laurel crown.

Celie had won!

Without taking her gaze off the crown, she bent down and put JouJou on the close-cropped turf. Her hands shaking, she reached out and picked up the crown.

There was a sound like a giant gong being struck, and everything tumbled about for a moment. Celie swayed, but still managed to put the crown on her head, where it fit perfectly. When everything settled, the maze was gone, and all the players were standing, blinking, in the sunlight, wondering which one of them had found the crown.

Celie couldn't speak, she just stood there with JouJou romping around her feet.

Then she heard Rolf shouting, "It's Celie! Celie has it! Hurrah!"

All the other players began to cheer, and Celie found her eyes swimming with happy tears. The next thing she knew, Bran and Rolf had made a chair with their arms and had scooped her up to carry her into the Castle.

"Celie is the winner!" Rolf was calling out everyone. "And now we can feast!"

"I won," Celie whispered, and Bran gently butted her head with his own.

"As if there was any doubt," Bran said.

JouJou barked happily, prancing in front of them toward the Castle.

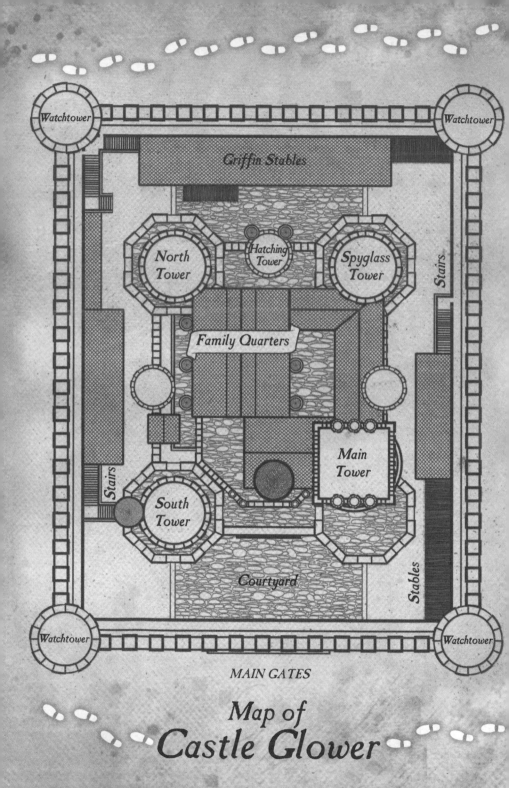

Map of
Castle Glower